CW01498655

Acknowledgements

Jayne Southern, editor extraodinaire, for her patience and fabulous sense of humour.

Anina and Jacques Stenvert, wonderful friends and an amazing design team. Thanks for the cover!

Laura and Justin for all your love and support and reading all my stories.

Laurence Cramer, for all the crits, advice and drinking till dawn. The bottles of Grants were worth it!

Prof Gérard Labuschagne of the SAPS Investigative Psychology unit for making sure I have all my facts straight.

Johan and Eileen, the best siblings a girl could ask for.

Thanks Mom – for everything!

And most of all, thanks to Adele Wearing, my tireless publisher. You're the best!

Requiem in E Sharp

Joan De La Haye

A Fox Spirit Original Novel

Fox Spirit Books
www.foxspirit.co.uk
adele@foxspirit.co.uk

ISBN:978-1-909348-15-8

Cover art by Jacques Stenvert
http://stenvert.co.za/

First Released July 2012

Distributed by Fox Spirit

To Johan
My big brother, who survived 17 bullets

1

His hands shook. He wanted them to stop; he wanted everything to stop.

All he could hear was her banging on the piano. It reverberated along the passage, through the tiled floor of his childhood bathroom and into his brain. The feel of the cold, smooth surface of the bath beneath his small curled-up body was soothing and calmed him. It was safe as long as she banged on the piano. The moment the music stopped the real nightmare would begin. Urine ran down the insides of his legs causing his jeans to cling to them. The music stopped. She would be coming soon.

He closed his eyes and tried to shut out the memory.

The car boot slammed shut and brought him back to the present. The street lights above his head flashed on and illuminated the quiet street. A slight though cool breeze played with crisp brown leaves on the ground around his feet; a dog barked down the street, disturbing the quiet suburb. The owner of the dog yelled at it to shut up. Why did people keep dogs to protect them, then stop them from doing their job? It was something he would never understand.

He watched her from the safety of his patrol car. She looked good in her jeans. She was well put together for a woman of her age, but it was on her face that time and alcohol told their story. Her short curly hair was tousled by the wind. He'd watched her for a few days, just as he'd watched the others. The memories flooded and overwhelmed him. They excited and horrified him. They all reminded him of that Bitch. She'd turned him into a monster.

The woman tried to pick up all the boxes piled around her feet. She hadn't had the brains to pack them flat, and her hands shook too much for her to be able to put them inside each other. Probably needed another drink. Getting out of his car, he slung his rucksack over his shoulder, checked that no one was around to identify him and walked through the open gate towards her. She never remembered to close the gate, probably to the disgust of the other inhabitants of the complex, but it suited his plans.

His hands stopped shaking and the noise in his head grew silent. All he saw was the woman who would soon be joining the others.

His footsteps crunched on the grass. He saw her back stiffen and heave as she took a deep breath before turning around. He sensed her fear and apprehension about being out alone in the dark. She looked around furtively, betraying the usual victim mentality in her every move. She was vulnerable and knew it, which excited him. Her body relaxed the moment she turned around and saw him coming towards her. The uniform always put them at ease. It was almost too easy.

He smiled, flashing his perfect teeth and asked "Hello Auntie, can I help you with those boxes?" His voice was calm and didn't betray the excitement he felt. He'd been taught that calling an older woman 'Auntie' was a sign of respect. Although he wasn't sure who'd taught him that – it certainly hadn't been his mother.

She nodded and smiled at him.

"You gave me a bit of a fright," she said with her hand over her thumping heart. He could see her willing it to slow down.

"I'm sorry. Didn't mean to," he said with his most sincere smile.

Adjusting the strap of his rucksack, he picked up most of the boxes, leaving two for her to carry and followed her towards the flats. The swimming pool in front of the block needed attention. Brown and gold leaves crunched under their shoes as they walked past the pool. The entrance of Queenswood Gardens was dark. The light above the door had blown and the caretaker hadn't replaced it yet. The pot plants on either side of the door had long since died. The sky turned from a dark blue to black and the thin crescent of the moon reflected in the pool.

They took the lift to the second floor. As the lift travelled slowly up she told him that she was moving to Cape Town and was looking forward to starting her life over. Getting away from all the bad memories would help in her recovery. Her high-pitched, sharp voice irritated him. Shutting her up would be a pleasure. He pictured her begging for her life. But then the woman's face turned into *hers*. He resisted the urge to kill her then and there. Anger welled up in the pit of his stomach. Only seeing her blood would keep that deep-seated anger and hatred from consuming him without pity or remorse. Not being shown pity was something he was used to. No-one had ever shown him pity before, so why should he be any different on himself or anybody else..

"Are you new to the block?" she asked. "I haven't seen you before."

He nodded. His mouth was dry and his hands were sweaty inside his gloves.

"Did you hear about what happened on the fifth floor?" she asked, sounding nervous.

He shook his head. He didn't trust himself to speak.

"Mrs Oosthuizen in five-oh-five caught her husband with the maid. I always thought he was one of *those*. She threw him out and now he's living with the maid in Mamelodi with the rest of the monkeys."

With that comment she'd made it a lot easier for him to kill her. One less narrow-minded, racist old cow was a service to the universe.

The lift door opened, he held it for her while she stepped out. She turned right into the passageway. The wind buffeted against the passage windows. She lived five doors down. He didn't take much notice of what number it was, but the door was in dire need of varnish. Inside, the walls needed a fresh coat of paint and the curtains demanded to be washed. The smell of stale cigarettes and booze hung in the air. The flat could also do with a bit of dusting. She was just like *her*: too lazy to clean up after herself.

She switched on the hall light. The bright light highlighted the dirty walls that hadn't been washed in years. Dirty hand-prints seemed to be her wallpaper of choice. He closed the door quietly behind him. Boxes in the lounge were in various stages of being packed. Piles of old newspaper littered the floor.

"Where do you want me to put these boxes for you?" he asked, his voice controlled.

"Just put them in the kitchen or you can just dump them here, please. I'll go take my jacket off and then make us a nice cup of coffee."

"Thanks," he replied. "But you really don't have to." He didn't want to drink her crappy coffee from her dirty chipped mug.

"Nonsense! I can't have you leaving here without having some coffee to warm you up first," she said, handing him the boxes she was carrying before walking down the narrow passage to her bedroom.

He turned left into the kitchen and dropped some of the boxes on the kitchen counter and some on the floor. An empty bottle of brandy lay comfortably on the top of her rubbish. His upper lip twitched as he scowled at the bottle and wondered how many more empty bottles were in the rubbish bin. While he waited for her, he surveyed his gloved hands and tried not to look at the empty bottle. *She* had given him the gloves for his birthday. They were one of the very few things she had ever given him. They were cheap black imitation leather and were starting to crack. He didn't know why he kept them, probably because they were a gift from *her*. The reason for hating them was also his reason for wanting to keep them.

He remembered one of the first presents he'd bought her with his own money as a child. It had been a pink fairy statuette for her bedroom. She'd thrown it away. He could still see the porcelain shards lying at the bottom of the trash can.

The woman returned to the kitchen while he was staring at the gloves. He hadn't noticed her come in. He snapped his head up and stiffened. He felt her watching him, judging him. Her eyes burned into him the same way that Bitch's eyes had burnt his soul. They had the same cold fish eyes, only hungry for the next drink. She turned to put the kettle on. His hand reached into the pocket of his jacket and felt the wire. He could feel the grooves and notches through his cheap gloves. He caressed it. He could feel his cock harden and his breath quickened in anticipation. He pulled the wire out of his pocket, savouring every second. He felt himself rushing the moment. He wanted to slow it down and enjoy every detail. But she would turn around any moment and things would get messy. He didn't want that to happen again. He wrapped the ends around his hands and pulled it taut.

He watched the back of her head bob up and down as she made the coffee, humming happily. The kettle was too loud. Her humming was out of tune and pulled his last nerve. She chatted about how rare it was to come across someone as polite as he was, but all he could hear was the sound of the piano clanging in his head. He crossed his wrists and slipped the wire over her head and pulled it around her throat. His heart lurched and the beat quickened. The excitement of the impending kill made him a little light-headed. A surprised groan escaped from her mouth. She tried to grab the wire, but her chewed fingernails were too short to dig in. She tried to grasp his gloved hands at the back of her head, but she was too slow. Her arms flailed around trying to hit him. Her foot connected with his shin. That would leave a bruise, he thought. He pulled the wire tighter. Its sharp edges cut into her flesh, slicing into her like a hot knife through butter. Her breath came in gasps; the more she struggled for breath the bigger and harder his erection grew. His breathing became harder and faster. The wire was swallowed up by her larynx. Blood ran down the front of her clothes. Her end was very close now, he could feel it. It was about time too. His muscles were killing him. The drunken old bitch had put up quite a fight.

Her struggle became feeble. She stopped fighting as her last breath left her and the wire cut through the arteries in her throat. Blood from the severed artery spray-painted the cupboard and his face. He felt her final breath escape. The sound of her last breath tickled his ear like a lover's whisper. Blood and spittle dribbled out of her mouth. He smothered the need to howl with pleasure as he came in his pants and allowed a loud moan to escape from between his lips.

Her body fell to the floor with a thump. Looking down at her, he thrust his gloved hand inside his pants. He felt the leatherette of the glove slipping against his cum as he rubbed his fingers against each other. Her blood and his sperm mixed on the leather. He fondled his now-limp penis, hoping to feel some flicker of excitement. Not even the thrill of having her blood on his cock excited him anymore. He felt nothing. He always hoped, with every victim, that he would feel something: something that would make sense. Something that would stem the flow of anger and hate he felt. But he never did and he would have to keep searching until he felt it.

Retracting his hand, he stared at the creaminess of his semen against the black of the glove. He slowly licked his fingers, relishing himself, savouring the sour, acrid tang that was his. He wondered if his diet really did affect its taste. He'd read that it did in some health magazine, but like most magazines they were probably full of shit.

He stared down at her body. Blood pooled around her head and his feet. It trickled into the grooves between the tiles, like red streams wending their way across the kitchen floor. He remembered the other two women who had taken *her* place. He'd killed them the same way and wished that each of them had been his mother; it was all her fault that these women were dead.

He remembered the first one he'd killed. It seemed so long ago now, but it had only been a couple of weeks. He'd watched her for months before he'd built up the courage to take action after that evil witch had gone after the only person he cared about. It had sent him over the edge. In a way, he'd hoped that someone would stop him – the cops, a random stranger walking past – but nobody did. They'd all been deaf, dumb and blind to his intentions.

His senses had been heightened during the time he'd stalked his prey. Everything tasted better and smells were so much more potent. Every sound was amplified as he followed her around Sunnyside.

Her block of flats was only a block away from where he lived. She'd been too drunk to even notice when he walked up behind her in her own flat. She'd left the door unlocked in her drunken state. But then it had become messy. She'd turned around at the wrong moment, which had been a surprise for both of them. Even in her drunken state she'd managed to put up a fight. She'd made him work for it. The fight had been over so quickly. Too quickly. None of it had gone the way he'd envisaged.

He'd wanted to savour every moment and had planned it all out in his head, only to be disappointed. He'd thought he would feel more, that he'd feel some guilt or remorse.

His lack of emotion was the only thing that had grieved him.

He'd hoped to feel more powerful or some sense that his mother's power over him was destroyed, but he'd felt nothing. Well, he'd heard the first one is always the hardest.

For days afterwards he'd thought that they'd catch him: every knock on the door had to be the cops. Maybe someone had seen him covered in blood. But the streets had been empty at that time on a Sunday night. The cops didn't show up on his doorstep. They were completely clueless. Considering that South Africa was literally one of the few countries where you could get away with murder, this shouldn't have been too much of a surprise. Every criminal knew that the police were just as corrupt as they, the felons, were. A couple of hundred rand would ensure the police docket disappeared. And then there were the incompetent forensic labs and the back log that was several years long. He'd recently watched a programme on Carte Blanche, the only news programme he bothered to watch, where the Forensic Pathologist office had been exposed. It took about three years for an autopsy report to be filed. The fact that they weren't knocking on his door shouldn't have been much cause for celebration.

The news coverage on the first one had been dismal but after the second one they'd paid attention. And now – he scrutinized the body at his feet – they would really pay attention. Three bodies were better than one.

He bent over, picked up her feet and dragged her through to her small closet-like bathroom. Her blood left a telltale trail behind him. The dark bathroom smelt of apples. A toilet flushed somewhere upstairs and the sound of the water rushed down to him through the open ventilation window. He dumped her in the bath tub and arranged her body so that it was in the foetal position, with her arms curled around her legs, switching on the bathroom light so he could admire his handiwork. The light flickered above his head and then flashed on, giving the scene a bright, harsh light. The room reminded him of the bathroom *she'd* locked him in, where he had so often cried himself to sleep, wet and cold, curled up in the tub. Conflicting emotions stirred within him. He felt triumphant, almost godlike staring down at his creation, but there was a part of him that wanted to scream out in pain at what he'd done. He shut his mind to the guilt that was making him weak.

He needed to urinate, so he stood over the bathtub, unzipped his pants and sprayed over her body. Relief flooded over him. The joy of pissing on a woman like her made him smile. When he was done he zipped himself up and left the bathroom.

He walked to the kitchen, leaving bloody footprints in his wake, retrieved his rucksack from the top of the kitchen counter and carried it back to the bathroom. He opened the bag and removed his digital camera. He placed himself at the edge of the tub, held the camera in front of him to find the best composition for his subject matter and took the picture. The body looked grotesque and scrunched up on the small screen, just the way he liked it. He thrust the camera back into the rucksack, put the plug in the bath and turned on the cold water tap. He watched the bath fill up while he cleaned the blood off his face, making himself look presentable and turned the tap off once the water was close to overflowing. The water turned red and the silence in the room made him feel serene. Her wet clothes ballooned around her body.

Closing the shower curtain, he picked up his rucksack and left the bathroom.

He smiled and started to whistle as he closed the front door behind him.

2

The sounds of Pretoria's streets drifted up to her through the open bedroom window. Tyres screeched and someone swore loudly before driving away. A man sang an African song in a language she couldn't understand, probably Sotho. His voice, a deep baritone, made her smile.

The capital city was experiencing another strange winter. Winter was generally the dry season with clear blue, cloudless skies and grass bleached white by the sun. But this year it hadn't stopped raining and the sky was anything but clear and cloudless. Today, however, it was sunny and a breeze played with the curtains.

Natalie almost jumped out of her skin when she heard Louis's keys in the door. The keys clanged as he threw them down on the kitchen counter. Heavy, quick footsteps came down the hallway towards her. She stopped brushing her long black hair and held her breath. She clenched the brush in her hands and the bristles bit into her skin. Moving from her vantage point at the window, she sat down at her dressing table. He stopped at the door and stood there, watching her. It always made her uncomfortable when he scrutinised her like that. She knew he would find fault with her. Turning around, she faced him and swallowed the fear germinating deep inside her. She had nothing to fear from him, she knew that, but couldn't help it.

His eyes were glacial and impossible to read. She always wondered what went on behind those cold, calculating eyes. He smiled and held out a bunch of roses. When he smiled at her like that she forgot everything. All she saw was that smile that held so much promise. She forgot the past and everything he had done to her, all the promises he'd broken. But her memory loss was temporary.

He walked across the room, put the roses on the table in front of her and stood behind her. They looked at each other in the small dressing table mirror. She felt him touch her hair and closed her eyes: he was always telling her how much he loved touching her hair. He ran his fingers through it like a comb, then bent over and placed a kiss on top of her head.

"Thanks for the roses," she whispered, worried that if she spoke it would break the spell. "They're beautiful."

"I know I'm not easy to live with but I do love you," he whispered into her hair.

She reached up, took his hand and kissed it, rubbed it against her cheek.

"And I love you," she whispered into his hand.

Taking his hand back, he straightened up, the moment of tenderness gone, without a trace. He wasn't comfortable with signs of affection. She should be used to it by now, but it always stung a little.

"Are you ready yet?" he asked, "They'll be here soon."

"Almost," she replied. Then, as an afterthought, "You don't mind that they're coming over, do you?"

"That's a fucking stupid question. Now, take your bloody flowers and put them in some water."

His mood swings were unpredictable. It was difficult to tell which way he would go and more often than not she guessed wrong.

Taking one last look at herself in the mirror she took the roses, went into the kitchen and put them in a vase with water. Her cat, Ginger, rubbed against her leg begging for food. She felt Louis's presence behind her as she arranged the roses. Ginger screeched as Louis booted her out of the kitchen. Natalie took a deep breath.

"Was that necessary?" she asked, as she spun around to face him.

From past experience, reacting like this meant she would get the boot as well as the cat, but time was on her side today. She looked up at the yellow plastic kitchen clock above her head. It was almost one o'clock. Janet should be here soon. Louis closed the distance between them in one stride and gripped her arm.

"Yes, it bloody was." He spat through clenched, even white teeth.

The intercom buzzed from the pedestrian gate downstairs. Louis released her arm.

"You better let them in," he said nodding towards the door. "I'll check on the fire and then join you guys in a minute."

She'd been looking forward to this afternoon and nothing Louis could do would ruin it for her. Even though she'd had second thoughts about it. But she pushed them aside. Janet was the closest thing she had to family and they hadn't seen each other since she'd tried to kill herself. Looking down at the still healing scars on her wrists she pushed the memories away, she focused on the present. Janet was introducing them to her new boyfriend. Natalie couldn't remember Janet ever having a serious boyfriend. There'd been lots of men she'd dated briefly and then discarded. This guy had to be special.

The lift was broken, so it would take them a few minutes to walk up to the third floor. It gave Natalie time to focus and compose herself.

Louis was on the balcony having a smoke when Janet and her man walked through the front door. Louis flicked the half-smoked cigarette over the railing and onto the street below, before joining them inside. He must have needed the nicotine to steady his nerves. Janet introduced the new man in her life as Nico. His handshake was firm and Janet's hug was warm and reassuring.

Louis must have used the paraffin again, Natalie thought, as she saw the roaring fire once they'd made their way to the balcony. Flames kissed wood and sent sparks flying into the air. Janet's bottle-blonde hair had just been cut to look like a young Meg Ryan. Frameless glasses were perched on the bridge of her slender nose. She'd always been beautiful and made Natalie feel like the ugly duckling. She'd compared herself to Janet when they were kids and always came up short and even now that they were adults, she still felt inadequate when standing next to Janet.

Nico was average in all senses of the word. He was chubby and his mousy hair was starting to recede. He was older than they were, by about ten years she guessed. The only things that Natalie noticed were his deep blue eyes: when he smiled it reached all the way to his eyes; so unlike Louis.

Janet and Louis made eye contact, acknowledging each other's presence. There was something veiled in the way they looked at each other. The way they interacted with each other had changed since the suicide attempt. It had once been warm and close, almost too close. But now they could barely handle being in the same room together without having a fight. She would have to watch them more closely.

Natalie leaned against the sliding door watching how Louis would react to Nico. Louis was dark and his features hard and angular in comparison with Nico's genial roundness. She chewed on her lip. If Louis didn't like him she wouldn't get to see a lot of Janet, which worried her, but then that nagging voice in the back of her mind asked if that was really such a bad thing? Could she trust Janet anymore? Could she trust either of them? Was any of it even true or was she letting that bitch get to her? As she watched them they seemed to get along and the voice at the back of her mind faded away. Louis could be friendly when he wanted and he seemed to be in a good mood now. Kicking Ginger must have helped.

There was only enough space on the balcony for the two men to sit, so she and Janet sat inside in the small but cosy lounge. She had tried to make it as comfortable as possible on their tight budget. She went to auctions and garage sales over weekends, always on the lookout for something that she could fix up and use to make the place look more attractive. Louis earned a pittance working for the armed reaction company; the fact that her boss was a tight-fisted bastard who expected her to work overtime – without pay – didn't help matters.

"So what's he like?" she asked Janet after they'd made their way through the usual boring pleasantries and were sitting comfortably on the couch. Lately, it seemed that all their conversations were made up of the usual boring pleasantries, always avoiding the giant elephant in the room.

"Well, he's sweet and gentle, but also strong. He makes me

feel safe," she paused. "He's a good man," she paused again, took a deep breath. Natalie had a feeling that she wasn't going to like whatever Janet was about to say. She didn't want to discuss that elephant. Any topic but the reason behind the tell-tale scars on her wrists.

"Nats, there's something I need to tell you about him. Please don't freak out."

"Why would I freak out?" Natalie couldn't help feeling a little insulted by that, but she was also relieved that it was about Nico and not about her and Louis.

"He's a cop," Janet said holding her breath.

Natalie's opinion of the police was anything but favourable. They all knew that and understood. Nobody could blame her for it after what had happened.

"He's a cop?" Natalie asked, crooking her thumb towards the balcony, a twinge of surprise in her voice mingled with a touch of anger which she struggled to control. "What are you thinking with? It certainly isn't your brain." Natalie couldn't help but remember her own experience with the police. They should have helped but all they ever did was protect the bastard who had raped her every night when she was a child. They'd made him the victim and her the criminal.

"Yes, he's a cop and it's not like that," she giggled and then looked seriously at her friend before taking a deep breath. "Besides, he's one of the good guys. I don't want to screw this up. I really like him. So please don't give me a hard time."

"Okay, as long as you know what you're doing. I'll try to give him the benefit of the doubt," Natalie said, then leaned forward and put her elbows on her knees, a strange glimmer in her eyes. "Have you done the deed yet?"

"Excuse me?" Janet asked. "That's a strange question coming from you. You've never been interested in my sex life before."

"I'm sorry. I'm just curious and besides, since when are you such a prude?"

"I'm not. It's just that I'm not used to someone wanting to take it slow. It's unfamiliar territory. Now, can we drop the subject, please?"

"So you haven't?"

"No, we haven't. Okay, you happy now? You didn't answer me before – why does my sex life, or should I say the lack of it, interest you so much now?"

"Sorry." She shrugged. "I didn't realise that you'd asked a question and misery likes company," she said, avoiding the real reason for her need to know that Janet was getting some action from a source other than Louis. "But we're not discussing Louis's temporary problem. Now don't change the subject. Why haven't you? Does he have the same problem as Louis?" She raised her index finger and dropped it. Keeping an eye on Janet's face for any signs.

"His equipment works just fine. We're taking our time, that's all." She took a deep breath and exhaled. "Natalie, are you okay?"

"I'm fine! Why?"

Janet's face was caring and gentle. The evil witch must have been lying.

"You're acting a little weird. Are you taking your pills?"

"Yes, I am taking my pills like a good little psycho. Don't worry; I have no intention of slitting my wrists again." She looked down again and examined the fresh red scars, still in the early stages of healing. The stitches had only been removed a week before. She'd acknowledged the white elephant. Hopefully it would now go away.

"I'm sorry Nats. It's just that I care about you. I don't want any of us to have to go through that again. Okay?"

"Okay! Just stop fussing. I'm a big girl and I can take care of myself. I can even tie my own shoelaces."

"Okay," Janet said while shaking her head. "You win. I'll shut up about it."

"Good to hear and I'm going to hold you to it."

Laughter floated through the open sliding door. Natalie looked at Janet and smiled.

"Well, they seem to be getting along," Natalie said.

"They should. They're both into playing cops and robbers."

Louis popped his head through the doorway and said, "Fire's just about ready for the meat, ladies, so we'll start braaing soon. How about some salad to go with it? That potato salad you always make so nicely would be quite *lekker*." His head was gone before she could come up with a snide comment.

Instead, Natalie sighed and said, "Typical, they get to drink beer and we have to make salad. Luckily the salad is almost made. I know my man too well."

"At least they're cooking the meat, one less thing for us to worry about," Janet replied.

Natalie stood up, walked into the small kitchen and opened the old fridge that Louis had bought from his mother. The only reason the evil witch had sold it to them was because she was too lazy to take it to the dump. It was far easier to make Louis buy it. The fact that they had been desperate had come in quite handy, for his mother anyway. The door almost fell off every time she opened it, but at least it worked. At this stage they couldn't afford to buy another one. The enamel was starting to chip; she would have to get some white enamel paint and cover up the black spots.

Louis's Black Labels were yet again clogging up the fridge. She always had to dig past them to get to her salad things. But most of all it annoyed her when she couldn't get to her gherkins without having to take out a six-pack. The fridge was big enough for his beer to go on another shelf, but no, he always put them in front of her gherkins. He knew she always put gherkins in her potato salad, which he always asked her to make. And he always put his bloody beer in front of them. Sometimes she thought he did it just to piss her off. On the other hand, he had the decency not to put them in front of her Prozac.

The potatoes were already cooked and chopped. All she had to do was the mayo sauce and boil an egg. Janet came into the kitchen and stood behind her. Natalie was aware of her watching and analysing everything she did. She picked up her bottle of Prozac, opened it, and popped one into her mouth. She took a sip of water straight from the tap and swallowed the pill. Janet sighed.

"See, I'm a good girl who takes her meds. Now stop being

such a mother hen. One would think you had something to feel guilty about," Natalie said, while putting the egg into the egg boiler and switching it on.

"That's a funny thing to say. What could I possibly have to feel guilty about?" Janet asked while trying to smile, but didn't quite succeed. She played with her hair, always a telltale sign that Janet was uncomfortable.

Natalie turned and grinned at Janet, "I was joking. Don't take everything so seriously. Instead of standing there watching me you could always butter those rolls you brought," she said. "Make yourself useful for a change." Her smile was forced and the kidding around wasn't as natural between them as it had once been.

They had just finished making the salad and buttering the rolls when Louis came in carrying the meat and placed it on the yellowwood kitchen table, which they had bought at a junk sale when they first moved in together. It had been an absolute bargain. A real find. Nico was close behind him carrying their Black Labels. Janet laid the table and Natalie placed the salad and rolls next to the meat.

"Hand me that big piece of steak and a piece of that *wors*," Louis said to Natalie. Louis' bad manners were legendary. They all knew and accepted that he hadn't been raised in a house where manners were on the agenda. Nico seemed to handle Louis' lack of grace. She took his plate and dished up as requested and added a roll and a large helping of potato salad.

"Don't be so stingy with the salad, babes," Louis said, as Natalie handed him his plate.

"Sorry!" she said and added another spoonful. Natalie served everybody else and, when everyone was busy tucking into their food, she dished a small portion up for herself.

As Nico took his first bite of his considerable T-bone steak, a cell phone rang. Louis and Janet checked to see if it was theirs.

"Van Staaden." Nico answered his cell phone with his mouth full of food. He nodded his head and swallowed "I'll be there in fifteen," he said. He looked up at everybody staring at him and said "Sorry folks, but we have to go."

"What?" asked Janet "What do you mean we have to go?"

"Sorry!" he said "They've found another body."

"Well, then we'll eat quickly, but another five or ten minutes won't make any difference to a dead body," Janet said while slicing into her rare steak.

Blood pooled on her white plate.

*

The smell of rotting flesh drifted on the wind. The odour of death was unmistakeable. Considering that the stench had reached him at the ground floor, he had to wonder how long the latest victim had gone undisturbed and why it took so long for anybody to report it. Yellow and black barrier tape marked the border of the crime scene, telling him that he had arrived at the right place. The smell was also at its strongest. The tape was strung along either side of the door to the flat, across the passageway. People stood in the small corridor on either side of the tape, pressing against each other, hoping to get a glimpse of the corpse. Most of them blocked their noses with their thumb and forefinger or tried to swat the smell away by waving their hands in front of their faces. Nothing they did would get that smell away. If they stood there long enough they'd never get it out of their clothes. He knew from experience. And yet they stayed to gawk. It amazed him.

Nico stepped under the tape and into the gap between the two groups of people, all vying to see into the apartment. He looked around him while he tugged the tight rubber gloves over his large hands. Why couldn't they make the gloves in different sizes? A young female constable, trying not to gag from the smell, was interviewing a middle-aged man wearing faded blue shorts. A pair of green plastic slipslops adorned the man's dirt-encrusted feet. His beer gut hung over the edge of his shorts. An old woman with her grey hair still in pink plastic curlers stood weeping at the edge of the crowd.

Nico knew that the scene inside would not be pleasant.

He hated this part of the job. He hated this case: the bloated dead bodies, and the smell of rotting flesh. There was nothing worse than a body that had been in water for a few days. It was a sight that would make the staunchest policeman lose his lunch. The thought made his stomach churn. He wanted this part over with but he had to get through this to do what he loved: catching the killer!

First things first.

All those people hanging around the scene had to go. He liked having the scene to himself. He needed to absorb it, to feel it; having all these bystanders around just messed with his concentration.

"Could we please clear the scene?" he asked a bored-looking constable standing at the edge of the void. The constable's attitude changed from bored to annoyed as he proceeded to ask people to go home.

Lazy bastard, Nico thought, this isn't a fucking picnic.

"There's nothing to see here, people. Go home. You're blocking the way. Please, people, let us do our jobs and go home. Have some respect for the dead," the constable said, showing very little respect towards the people around him.

Nico took the plastic shoe covers out of his jacket pocket and pulled them over his shoes. The elastic band at the top closed around the hem of his pants. The covers prevented him from carrying in anything that could contaminate the scene any more than it already had been. The forensic team would go through the place with a fine-toothed comb once he was finished. They would probably rip the place to shreds. It would never look the same again. Which was probably a good thing. The protective shoe covers rustled on the ground as he walked. The smell of rotting human flesh assaulted his nose as he went inside the small two-bedroom flat. The profiler on the case, Dr. Pete Papenfuss from the Investigative Psychology Unit, and the police photographer, Thabiso Ngweni, were waiting for him at the door. They already had Vicks vapour rub under their noses to cover up at least some of the smell drifting up their nostrils. Toothpaste also worked.

"Thank you for finally deigning to join us, Captain Van

Staaden," Pete said, with a wolfish grin that showed off his yellowing teeth. Too much coffee and nicotine hadn't done his teeth any favours.

"Why do they always have to find the bodies on a Sunday?" Nico asked. "Ruined a perfectly good lunch."

"I think they do it just to irritate us." Thabiso chipped in.

"Looks like she was in the process of moving," Nico said, looking at the boxes in the hall and strewn across the lounge.

They walked the scene, each one taking notes and making their own observations. One of them would notice something that the others could miss. Three pairs of eyes were better than one. He tried to forget that the other two were with him and absorbed everything that was around him. They started at the front door and worked their way through the flat. Thabiso took pictures of anything that could be possible evidence. They climbed over the boxes and examined the contents in each.

In the kitchen they found the two coffee cups. The milk jug was still standing next to the coffee that would never be drunk. The milk had turned sour. The smell of the sour milk was overpowered by that of the corpse. Blood, coagulated on the counter, had also run down the cupboards and collected in a small puddle at the base. A trail of blood led from another larger puddle, where her head had fallen, out of the kitchen door towards the bathroom. The boxes were still on the kitchen counter and on the floor, decorated by blood from her severed artery. There was an empty bottle of brandy lying on its side on top of the full rubbish bin. Thabiso snapped a few shots from a 90-degree angle and from all four corners of the room so that nothing would be missed. One cupboard door below the counter was hanging at an angle. It looked as though it had been kicked. Scuffmarks were visible.

"Signs of a struggle." Dr. Papenfuss said, pointing at the cupboard.

"She was even making him a cup of coffee. Son of a bitch."

"At least she put up a struggle," Thabiso chipped in once again.

Nico and Pete turned and looked at him and shook their heads.

"She's still dead," Nico said.

"Maybe the forensic guys will be able to get something off those," Thabiso said, tilting his head at the coffee cups and milk.

"Keep dreaming," Nico replied. "Our boy wouldn't have been stupid enough to drink out of the cup. Plus, by the time we get the results there'll be several more corpses to deal with."

Nico stared at the scuffmarks and tried to put himself in the killer's place. Tried to feel what the killer had felt. It was dark and lonely. He thought about Janet, her blue eyes and soft skin. She pulled him out of the darkness. But he needed to linger there a while longer and pushed her image out of his mind.

In the bedroom they found a crumpled jacket lying on the bed. A small wooden crucifix hung on the wall above it. A wedding photo in an old silver frame stood on the bedside table: an attractive couple smiling at each other, obviously in love. A sign of happier times. The bedroom was curiously peaceful, undisturbed by violence and death.

It was in the bathroom, however, that they encountered the reason for giving up their Sunday. The body was bloated and the skin was starting to fall away from the muscle tissue. The water had done its damage. Her clothes had given her body some protection, but parts of her, like her hands, neck and head were badly decomposed. The flesh was falling off the bones of her fingers and the portion of her head that wasn't submerged in the water had turned black. The water itself was murky and a ring of slime had formed around the rim of the bath.

"She's been lying in the water for about a week, I'd guess. Thanks to the water there's not much hope of finding any forensic evidence and the Forensic Pathologist won't be able to give you the exact time of death," Pete said, standing over the bath and examining the woman's body. Nico leaned over the bath to get a closer look. The smell made his bile rise.

"She was garrotted, the same as the other two. Our killer's been a busy boy. Any idea who this one is?" asked Nico.

Pete consulted the small notebook he always carried with him and said, "Her name was Theresa van Wyk, divorced with no children. Her neighbour complained about the smell, so the caretaker let himself in. He got a bit of a surprise when he came in here."

"I bet he did. Is he the guy in the shorts with very dirty feet?"

"That's him."

"Did he touch anything?"

"He says not."

Pete looked at the shower curtain. "I wonder if he opened the curtain to find the body," he said, almost to himself while taking notes.

"Remind me to ask him when I interview him," Nico replied while fingering the curtain.

The photographer snapped some more shots of Mrs van Wyk's body, curled up in the foetal position. Her jean-clad legs were pulled up to her chest and her body suspended in the murky bathwater. It was a sad and profane parody of new life. Was that what the killer was after? A new life?

The photographer took photos from every corner in the room, as he had in the kitchen.

"Okay," Nico said to Pete. "Recap time. What do we know about this guy?"

"For one thing he's organised. He brings everything with him, his so-called killing kit. He targets older women; probably has mommy issues. He's a young white male, probably mid-to late-twenties. Has knowledge of police procedure and could be in law enforcement. He also has no respect for our abilities to catch him. He makes no attempt to cover up his crime. Oh yes, and he's a big boy, probably about six foot."

"How do you know how big he is?" Thabiso asked between snapshots.

"Didn't you see the size of those bloody shoe prints in the passage?" Nico asked, his tone harsh and irritable.

"Plus these women are not exactly small. A small guy

wouldn't be able to pick them up very easily." Pete said, interjecting before Nico and Thabiso could get into another argument.

"And how do you know that he's a white boy or that he's a cop?" Thabiso asked, ignoring the look on Nico's face. "That's a bit racist isn't it?"

"A witness saw a young white male in what could have been a police uniform leaving the first victims apartment," Pete said.

"Why do you want to know about the shower curtain?" Nico asked, fingering the curtain the way Pete had done earlier.

"The others were closed. If he closes the curtain it means he does feel some remorse for what he's done. If he left this one open, then something's changed and something we need to know about."

Nico nodded his head and mulled everything over, but came up empty. He had no answers, only more questions. He needed space and time alone. The flashes from the camera irritated him.

"Hey," Nico clicked his fingers at Thabiso whose name he had trouble remembering. "Um, why don't you go take some photos of the crowd in the passage and outside the building?"

"I already did that while we were waiting for you. I guess I'm a little more with it than you are today." Thabiso was offended. "Oh, and by the way, my name is Thabiso, but I'll go take some more shots of the ones still hanging around just to make the *baas* happy." He left, mumbling to himself.

"Well, I guess I just put my foot in that one," Nico said and turned back to Mrs van Wyk's floating body.

"He'll get over it. He's a good guy and good at his job. You really should try and get on with him. Remembering his name might be a good place to start," Pete said.

Mrs van Wyk's open, dead eyes looked back at Nico. The irises were now a smoky-white. He wondered what colour her eyes used to be. Her mouth was slightly open, probably from the last breath she had exhaled.

"I'll leave you alone, so you can have your conversation

with her, or what ever it is you do. I'll give you five minutes before I send the forensic boys in," Pete said and left the room.

"*Ja, ja*. Piss off." His focus was on Theresa van Wyk; he hardly noticed the doctor leave. He sat on the toilet, next to the bath and looked down at the rotting body in the bath.

"So … Theresa, why did he kill you? What made you his target? Who do you remind him of?"

But the woman would never answer him, stubbornly mute in her noxious, amniotic grave. He was still sitting in that position, staring at the body, when the forensic guys started collecting samples of the bath water to be analysed at the lab. He wandered how long those results would take. The backlog at the lab was monumental and incredibly frustrating for any cop trying to solve a case. Detectives were working with one hand tied behind their backs.

He left the flat while they emptied the water out of the bath and with great difficulty moved her body onto the gurney. Her saturated clothes didn't make it any easier.

Once outside the flat he took a deep breath. The air outside was fresher and a welcome antidote to the smell of rotting flesh. He took the lift down to the ground floor, where the circus was waiting for him. Inquisitive people from the neighbourhood had gathered outside the building. Didn't these people have anything better to do on a Sunday afternoon than turn someone's death into an event?

The flash of a press photographer taking a snapshot almost blinded him. Thabiso was hard at work taking snapshots of potential suspects in the crowd, hanging around to soak up the aftermath of his handiwork. A blonde woman from the SABC news team shoved a microphone in his face.

"Well, if it isn't Helen Stratford," Nico said, pushing the microphone out of his way. The memory of her, naked and laughing, flashed through his mind. Instantly making him feel guilty.

"Hello, Nico. You're not still angry with me, are you?" she asked, giving him her most alluring smile. It always worked on him, or it had in the past.

"Why would I be?"

"I don't know. Maybe because …"

He interrupted her before she could finish.

"Look Helen, I'm working and if I remember correctly, our problems were because of our jobs. You were dedicated to getting the story no matter who was hurt, even if it meant screwing me over."

"So you are angry."

"It's ancient history. Now, if you don't mind, I do have a case to work."

"Speaking of the case, is it the Bathroom Strangler?"

"Sorry Helen, you know I can't give you anything yet."

"Come on Nico. For old time's sake?"

"No, not even for you," he said as he pushed past her. He needed to get away from her. She always managed to get to him he thought, as he realised his hands were shaking and his heart was pounding.

He looked around, searching for something out of place, and moved his mind off Helen and back where it belonged, on the case. The streets were quiet, only the usual Sunday afternoon traffic in the suburbs. A blue Citi Golf drove past, slowed down to gawk at the spectacle, then carried on driving. A few cars were parked in the parking lot and on the dying grass. It was while absorbing this information that he noticed the Rent-a-Cop patrol car parked across the road between a dented, red Volkswagen Beetle and a white Golf Chico. He walked towards it. The driver got out and started to walk towards him. As the man drew closer Nico recognised him. It was Louis.

"Howzit? What are you doing here?" he asked Louis.

"I had to work. The guy who usually works this shift called in sick and here I am. Nats isn't too happy about it, but we need the cash. So is this the reason that you had to leave?"

"Uh-huh. I don't suppose you were working in this area last Sunday?"

"I had the Sunday night shift. Why?"

"See anything strange? Anybody hanging around?"

"You mean other than me?" He laughed. It was a forced

laugh that sent tingles along Nico's nerves. "What time on Sunday?"

"Unfortunately we still don't know what time she was killed. Sunday's also a bit of guess at this stage."

"Then I'm sorry, bro, but I can't help you there. But I do have another idea. How about we get together for a beer in a couple of hours?"

"Sounds like a plan. I could fit in a short and very welcome break. But aren't you on duty?"

"*Ja*, but one beer's not going to make much of a difference to my ability to check on a bogus alarm. I leave the important crime solving to your brothers in uniform."

"Okay," Nico laughed. "As long as it doesn't get you fired. How about we meet at five at News Café in Hatfield?"

"Sounds good. I'll see you then." Louis turned and walked back to his car. Nico watched him. There was something that wasn't right about the guy, but he'd promised Janet that he'd give him a chance, so he pushed his misgivings aside for the time being.

*

He watched the crime scene from the safety of his car. The young black photographer was snapping photos of the crowd standing in front of the building. He wondered what the woman's corpse would look like now. How did she smell? Was her flesh falling away from her brittle bones? Was she being held together by her clothes? He wished it was *that* Bitch. If only *she* was the one decomposing. The thought gave him an erection. He watched a well-dressed blonde woman get out of the SABC TV News van.

Well, well, he thought, I'm going to be on the news tonight. The coverage on the first murder had been abysmal. The second one had created a satisfying buzz. This one would get their attention. He watched the SABC newswoman hijack the Captain on the case. Good old Nico van Staaden, who was looking a little flustered. They looked like they knew each other. Interesting. Maybe it was something he could use to his advantage.

"Having a bad day, my friend?" he mumbled to himself.

While the police asked bystanders questions and more press arrived, he stuck his hands inside his pants and touched his erect penis. He thought about how it would feel to strangle *her*. He wondered how it would feel to hear that witch struggle for her last breath. With each thought his erection grew harder. Maybe he would kill her tonight, he thought, with a smile.

3

Hatfield, Pretoria's main social spot, was bustling with life. Not a day went by when there weren't hordes of people drinking and laughing in the suburb. News Café on a Sunday afternoon was packed with an assortment of people. A mix of students, yuppies and flea-market bargain hunters sipped cocktails while the sun set. Muffled voices and clinking glasses filled the air. A man's drunken voice rose above the others shouting for another beer.

Louis sat at the bar drinking his Black Label and kept one eye on the door. The bar counter was still wet from the barman's alcohol-soaked cloth. A young woman, probably a student at TUKS, wearing a pair of skin-tight denim hipsters walked past him and gave him the once-over. He noticed she changed her walk to accentuate her rear end. He chuckled. . Taking another sip of his beer, he admired the show and thanked his lucky stars that Nats wasn't there to see it. She would have scratched her eyes out

Someone sat down on the bar stool next to him. The sound of the stool clanging against the brass foot rail made Louis jump. It was Nico, not his jealous girlfriend.

"Howzit Bro! I didn't even see you come in," Louis said.

"*Ja*, I saw your attention was elsewhere, so I took the chance to sneak up on you. It's what we cops are good at."

"Okay, if you say so," Louis laughed. "So can I buy you a beer?"

"That would be great. Thanks."

Louis got the bartender's attention and ordered a Black Label for Nico and another for himself. Louis tapped the counter with his fingers and looked around the crowded bar, trying to think of something to say while they waited for the beer to arrive.

"So," he eventually decided on, "any closer to finding this so-called ... um ... what did the press call him again?"

"The Bathroom Strangler?"

"Yes, that's the one. So any idea who he is?"

"Nope, and I really shouldn't be discussing the case with anybody."

"Come on," Louis said, looking eager for more information. You've got to tell me about it. I promise I won't tell anybody."

"I don't know."

"Look, if you don't trust me, then that's fine. You don't have to tell me anything. It's okay. We'll just drink our beers. I thought that maybe talking about it might help you clear things up in your own head. You never know you might have one of those eureka moments, but if you'd rather not, I understand ... I'm not a member of the club."

"What club?"

"The Cop Club," Louis said, using his fingers as inverted commas.

"There's no such club. Trust me. It's not that I don't trust you. It's just that it's embarrassing that we have so little to go on; we're still busy pulling all the evidence together. I don't want to bore you with the details."

"You couldn't possibly bore me. I find this fascinating ... It's all anybody in the control room at work talks about."

"Seriously? Don't they have anything better to do?"

"Nah, all they used to worry about was who was shagging whom. At least now it's interesting. So, aren't you any closer to finding him?"

"We're working on it. We've got a few leads we're looking into."

"Well, that's good. Maybe you'll catch him before the next one."

The look on Nico's face told him it was doubtful.

"We live in hope one of the leads will pan out and will break the case," Nico said.

Louis laughed. He couldn't help himself.

"So, that's the party line is it?" Louis asked with an ambiguous smile.

"I'm afraid so," Nico said and took a swig from his beer.

"That's okay. I understand. Janet told me about what happened with your ex. If I were in your shoes, I'd also be careful about who I discussed things with."

"Janet told you about Helen?" Nico almost spat out his beer.

"*Ja*, we tell each other everything. Have done since we were kids. No secrets in our group." Louis sipped his beer and wondered if he should have said that. The look on Nico's face was not encouraging.

"That's good to know." Nico swallowed a large gulp of beer.

Just as Louis was about to ask Nico another question, Nico's cell phone rang.

"Sorry, I have to take this," he said with a slight sigh of relief and answered, "Van Staaden".

Nico nodded his head a few times.

"Okay, I'll be there as soon as I can," he said to the person on the other end. Turning back to Louis, he said, "That was the Forensic Pathologist. It seems he's ready to talk to me now. I'm sorry to cut this short but duty calls."

"Sure, not a problem, maybe we can do this some other time. I know the girls want us to be friends."

"Okay-*ja*-no-well-fine. Give me a shout some time and we can make a plan."

Nico walked out of the bar leaving Louis still sitting on his stool and with the bill. Louis took a final swig of his beer with a grimace and paid for the beers. Things hadn't gone quite as he'd hoped.

"Well, I guess I'd better visit my mother," he muttered to himself as he left.

*

Walking into his mother's flat brought back too many memories. Hardly any of them good. Why he put himself through this every Sunday he would never know. He picked up the old photo of his parents on their wedding day. It had been standing on his mother's dusty piano ever since his father left.

He would never forget that night. The sounds of his parents fighting in the lounge had woken him up.

"I don't want you or that bastard of yours!" his father yelled. "I'm not even sure he's mine! You're just a fucking whore! You're both good for nothings!"

Tears ran down his face as he snuck out of his bedroom and down the dark passage. His bare feet didn't make a sound on the cold tiles. He peered around the wall and saw his mother holding a full whisky glass, emptying the contents into her mouth. His father picked up his packed bags and walked out of the house and out of his life. He watched in shock as his mother threw the empty whisky glass at the shut door. She turned around and saw him standing there. He tried, unsuccessfully, to make himself invisible.

"You!" she shouted, "It's all your fault! If it weren't for you he'd still be here!" In a matter of seconds she had grabbed him by his pyjama collar and dragged him to the bathroom. She flung him in. He skidded across the cold smooth floor and cracked his head on the bathtub. She kicked him over and over again. Everything went black.

Hours later he woke up in the bathroom on the cold floor with his legs wet and sticky. The slightest movement caused him pain. He remembered that his father was gone. His father didn't want him any more and his mother hated him.

The sound of his mother calling him from the kitchen brought him back to the present. He was no longer the scared little six-year-old boy but a thirty-one-year-old man.

"Louis, is that you?" his mother screeched from the kitchen.

"*Ja*, Ma," he yelled back as he walked through the small dirty house towards the kitchen. He poked his head round the door.

"You're late," she said.

"Sorry, Ma." He looked down at his feet.

"But what else could I expect from you, hey?"

"Yes Ma. Sorry Ma." He examined his feet more closely. He should have polished his shoes: she would notice. He rubbed the tip of his left shoe up and down on his calf, hoping that his jeans would some how manage to give his shoes that just-polished shine. He then did the same to his right shoe.

"What are you doing hopping around like an idiot?" His mother had caught him, she always did.

"Nothing, Ma."

"That's the problem with you. You're always doing nothing. You just stand there looking like an idiot. Make yourself useful for a change and make your poor mother a cup of coffee."

"Yes Ma." He put the kettle on and took a mug out of the cupboard above his head. His mother walked out of the kitchen and waited to be served her coffee in the lounge. He poured the boiling water into the mug, added a heaped teaspoonful of Frisco and three spoons of sugar. No milk. Her coffee was as black as her heart. He carried the hot coffee through to the lounge, careful not to spill a drop.

She sat on the couch with her legs crossed. He could still see the attractive woman she had once been beneath the wrinkles and the overdone make-up. He'd need a knife to scrape the gunk off her face to see what she really looked like. He put the coffee down in front of her and sat down on the edge of the opposite couch. She took a sip and immediately spat it out.

"What kind of crap coffee is this?" she asked as she smacked the mug down on to the dusty and now wet table.

"It's how you always drink it, Ma."

"Are you trying to poison me? After everything I've done for you."

"No, Ma," he said. "I can make you another cup if you don't like that one."

"No, you'll just try to poison me again. Pour me a strong drink instead. At least you won't be able to put poison in my whisky with me watching you like a hawk."

"Ma, how many times do I have to tell you that I'm not trying to poison you? … nobody is. You're imagining things."

"Don't back chat me, little boy. Just pour me my fucking drink."

"Yes Ma. Sorry Ma."

He stood up and walked over to the small battered cupboard that served his mother as her liquor cabinet. He took out the bottle of Three Ships Whisky and poured a triple tot into a dirty glass standing on top of the cabinet. He put the glass down in front of her. She picked it up and threw the contents down her throat. Wiping her mouth with the back of her hand, she handed the glass back to Louis.

"Pour me another one and make it stronger this time."

He poured her another triple shot and gave her the glass without a word.

"Don't look at me like that, Louis," she said and downed the alcohol. "I deserve a little bit of respect after everything I've sacrificed for you. I'm all alone because of you and you want to desert me just like your father."

"No, Ma, I'm not going to desert you. I'm here every Sunday, aren't I?"

"But you would love to desert me just like your father, wouldn't you?"

"No, Ma. You're the only mother I have and I love you."

"Show me how much you love me and pour me another drink."

He took the glass from her and poured her another drink.

"Good boy," she said when he gave her the glass. "Give your mother a kiss and then get lost. I've seen enough of your ugly face."

He bent over and kissed her on her forehead.

"No. Kiss me properly."

He bent over and kissed her on the lips. Her tongue slithered into his mouth. He tasted the whisky and wanted to throw up. He managed to extract himself from her vice-like grip on the nape of his neck before he gagged.

He turned, wiped his mouth with the back of his hand and walked towards the dark passageway that led to the front door. He stopped at the piano. It was incongruous. It didn't fit in with the other furniture, which was all bargain-basement stuff; it certainly wasn't compatible with the woman he knew to be his mother.

The piano had belonged to his father. His father had taught his mother to play when they first met but she now only thumped on it when she was drunk. She always thumped out the same piece of music, the last piece his father had tried to teach her to play, a Rachmaninoff piece, which his mother called the 'coffin concerto'. As he closed the door behind him he heard his mother start to bang on the piano. The sound tarantella'd up his spine.

It sounded like knocking from the inside of a closed coffin.

4

Nico arranged to meet the Forensic Pathologist in the Government Mortuary. The smell of industrial strength disinfectant hung in the air. The mortuary was kept clean and sterile judging by how the surfaces seemed to sparkle. The sparkling almost belied the fact that the only thing to be found in this basement was a bunch of dead people. He thought it was strange that it was cleaner here, where they kept these dead bodies, than many hospitals where people were fighting to stay alive.

The Forensic Pathologist, Dr. Michael Keartland, was standing over Theresa van Wyk's corpse with Dr. Pete Papenfuss when Nico walked into the mortuary. Her clothes had been peeled off her flesh slowly and carefully to limit the damage but despite this, some of her skin was stuck to her jeans and jersey, leaving behind bloody meat and bone. What was left of her body had been cleaned and was in the process of being autopsied. The case had been bumped to the front of the queue.

A Y-incision had been made in Theresa van Wyk's chest and her ribcage had been removed using garden pruning shears. He was relieved he would miss the rest of the autopsy. He saw enough blood and guts everyday – he didn't need to see an entire post-mortem as well.

"Have you two discovered anything interesting?" Nico asked from the door. They looked up from the body.

"Well, I've found out what kind of wire your Bathroom Strangler's been using," said a very proud Pete.

"That's good news. What kind of wire is it?"

"I know how you hate all the technical information, so I called the forensic guys for you."

"Thanks, you get brownie points for that. Now tell me what kind of wire it is?"

"Patience is a virtue, but it's piano wire: E sharp to be exact, also commonly referred to as F natural. The old codger in the lab is insisting that in his day it was referred to as E sharp and that it should stay that way."

"Okay ... interesting. But how the hell did they figure that out?"

"They've been experimenting with different wires up until now and they found a microscopic piece still stuck inside Michelle Venter's throat, the first victim. It's a miracle that it was still there, considering how long she was in the water. Anyway, the bit that they found in this lady over here," he said pointing down at Theresa van Wyks's naked body on the metal slab, "just confirmed their suspicions."

"Okay Doc, I get the picture. Why are you so sure that it's piano wire? Couldn't it just be any old kind of wire?"

"It's possible, but the flake they found has the same consistency as piano wire. Besides which, piano wire is the best type of wire for garrotting, especially E sharp. It's thin and sharp and cuts through clay very nicely, apparently. Plus the way the wire slit all the victims' throats is almost an exact match to the way the E sharp wire cut through the mounds of clay they used in the lab."

"So that's how they experiment with different types of wire?" Nico asked him.

"That's right. They used clay as a substitute for the human body.

"Thanks again, Doc. Is there anything else?" Nico asked Pete.

"Yes, I have a little something for you." He reached into his jacket pocket and pulled out a piece of coiled wire. "I thought you might want to see an example of what the wire looks like and put it up on your wall of horror."

"Thanks, Doc. Is that everything?"

"I think so, but I'll let you know if I find anything else."

"Good." And then turning to the Forensic Pathologist, "Please tell me you also have something and that you're going to make my life considerably easier."

"Nothing quite as exciting as Dr Papenfuss here," said the Pathologist. "But judging by the angle of the cut he was quite tall, approximately six feet and, like the other victims, she wasn't raped. No signs of vaginal tearing or subcutaneous bruising that would indicate a rape or any other kind of sexual activity. That's about all I can tell you. The time she spent in the water destroyed any other evidence as well as messing with the time frame. So I can't give you an estimate as to the time of death. I'll have the results from the blood work in a few days if we're lucky and I'll be able to tell you more then."

"I guess I'll just have to work on my patience and wait for the lab," he said while shaking his head. "Well, thank you, doctors, for your help. Now I just have to do some old-fashioned detective work."

*

Natalie sat at the kitchen table chewing her nails. She watched the front door from her perch, expecting it to open with every second that ticked past.

She hated Sundays.

At least the day had started off well in spite of the dead body interrupting their lunch. She glanced at the yellow kitchen clock. Eight o'clock: he should be back any moment now. She drummed her fingertips on the chipped wooden surface and then combed her fingers through her hair, noticed split ends and bit them off. The minutes carried on ticking by.

She was still staring at the clock half an hour later when the keys rattled in the lock. She bolted from her seat and stood in the kitchen doorway nibbling on her fingers, waiting for him. She recognised the look on his face the moment he walked through the doorway. It was the same look he had almost every Sunday night. He closed the door behind him and pushed past her into the kitchen. He opened the fridge, took out a beer and slammed the door shut. Natalie stayed planted in the doorway. Louis downed the beer and then exhaled.

"So how's your mother?" Natalie asked, leaning against the doorframe.

"The same as she always is. Cruel and mean," he said, grabbing another beer out of the fridge. Again he slammed the door shut and pushed past Natalie on his way out of the kitchen.

"Then why do you go every Sunday, especially after everything she's done to us?" she asked, following him out of the kitchen.

"She's still my mother and if you had ever had a mother you would know that blood is thicker than water. Now please, Nat, not now. I'm not in the mood for one of your little tantrums."

"What is that supposed to mean?"

"What is what supposed to mean?"

"The whole blood-is-thicker-than-water crap and I'm not throwing a tantrum."

"Just shut up. I'm not in the mood for this. I might as well have stayed at my mother's if this is how you're going to be."

"No. I will not shut up. Why do you always have to shove not having parents in my face?" Tears started to fall down her cheeks.

"For fuck's sake Natalie, just stop with the waterworks. I get enough of that crap from my mother. I sure as hell don't need it from you, especially not tonight."

"You wish I'd done it properly, don't you?"

"What the fuck are you talking about now?"

"The night I slit my wrists. You wanted me to die, didn't you? You wanted me gone so you could be with Janet."

"Just stop right there. You don't know what you're talking about. I don't want to be with Janet. I never have"

"Liar!" She screamed at him, pushing him, but she couldn't stop herself. She knew which buttons to press. She was alive when she felt pain – any pain, be it mental, emotional or physical. Pain was her friend. "Well, I'm sorry I didn't die. I'm sorry you have to deal with having me in your pathetic little life."

She knew she was on the verge of being hysterical and felt the back of his hand slam into her cheek. The familiar stinging sensation brought her back from the edge. Her tears ran down over the red welt developing on her pale cheek. He struggled to maintain control and clenched and unclenched his fists. She stood rooted to the floor. Sobs racked her body.

"Don't ever say that again. I never want to hear you utter those words ever again. Do you hear me?" he shouted and shoved his index finger in her face.

She had nothing left to say. Her only response was a gut wrenching sob. He pushed her out of his way, forcing her to fall to the floor, and stepped over her. The front door slammed behind him. She heard him rev the engine of his battered Toyota Tazz followed by the squeal of tyres as he drove out of the parking lot below.

Lying on the cold kitchen floor, memories of the night not so long ago flooded over her. Louis's mother had paid her an unexpected and unwelcome visit. The evil cow had taken great relish in telling her all the sordid details about Louis's sexual escapades with Janet and with one other person. Oh god, she groaned. It was just too horrible to think about: the betrayal was too much to bear.

How could they pretend to love her when they were doing *that* behind her back? She didn't remember how the knife had appeared in her hand. She didn't remember what else his mother said. All she knew was when she sliced into her wrists and the blood seeped out of her veins, the agony stopped. The noise in her head was silenced. It was the most peaceful she'd ever felt. Even that evil woman's cruel laughter didn't bother her.

She'd woken up in the hospital with Louis standing over her. He'd promised that things would change. Empty promises. Nothing had changed.

Ginger slinked out of whatever hiding place she'd been in and rubbed herself against Natalie and purred.

*

The photographs of the Bathroom Strangler's victims adorned the walls of the operations room assigned to the task team investigating the killings. All the women were in their mid-fifties, garrotted and found floating in their baths. Nico's skin crawled every time he walked into the room. It was no different on this Monday morning. He couldn't help wondering when the next body would be found. The fact, according to the killer's profile and a witness statement, he was one of their own just pissed him off even more.

He walked up to the wall opposite the door, where most of the pictures were displayed. The wall was divided into the different murder scenes. In the middle of each group of pictures was a blown-up headshot of the women before they were murdered. Next to that were pictures of the victims, taken at the mortuary, of their heads and shoulders. It was a 'before and after' collage. Around those were smaller snapshots of the individual crime scenes. He felt as if he knew each of the victims personally. He knew he had to distance himself from them but he couldn't. They all reminded him of his mother: her killer had never been brought to justice.

He heard the rest of the policemen and women who made up the task team filing into the room behind him. Papers shuffled and desks scraped as they found their seats. Any of them could be the killer. He turned around and watched them drinking coffee and chatting as though they didn't have a care in the world. He would never be able to understand how they could just shut out the horror on the walls encircling them. Then again, maybe he was someone who felt too much.

He raised his voice above the chatter and scraping of chairs as they started to take their seats.

"Okay boys and girls, we have another body to add to the list. Her name is Theresa van Wyk. Fifty-five years old and divorced. No news on hubby. Steon, that's your job. Track him down and find out where he was and all the usual bullshit. Thanks," Nico said, pointing at an overweight policeman at the back of the room. "The Forensic Pathologist isn't able to give us a clear idea of the exact time of death. Closest we can guess is last Sunday. The Forensic Pathologist has also determined the killer is about six-foot tall due to the angle of the incision. According to her neighbour, a sweet old lady called Mrs Du Plessis, the victim went out to do her shopping at the local Spar in Kilnerpark and to fetch some more boxes for packing. That was the last time she was seen in the land of the living. No one remembers seeing her there. Frank and Lucas: canvas the area again. Maybe they've remembered something since yesterday. Bother them at work, maybe that'll jog their memories. Someone out there has to have seen something. Okay, we now know what kind of wire he's using, thanks to our forensic team. It seems our boy likes piano wire. He's using the E sharp wire to garrotte these ladies. So start checking up on piano shops and people who can fix these things. Apparently it's quite a specialised field. Any questions?" he asked, looking around the room with his hands behind his back. "Nothing? Our boy seems to have a thing about Sundays so we probably have less than a week before the next body turns up. This is the third body, so we officially have a serial killer on our hands. Which means there's going to be a lot of pressure from the press and the brass so we need to wrap this up as soon as possible and put him away. Remember this guy is killing every week like clockwork. Let's just hope he sticks to that and doesn't decide to accelerate his spree and kill every day. That's all. Now get out there and kindly catch me the murdering SOB. Watch your backs; we don't want any of your pictures on this wall."

He watched them leave the room and wondered which they would find first: another dead body or, by some miracle, the killer.

If he was a gambling man he would have bet on the corpse.

5

Natalie couldn't sleep. She was lying on her back in their bed with the duvet pulled up to her chin. The wind buffeted against the windows. The street lights outside the bedroom window caused shadows to form on the walls. She watched them dance to a strange rhythm. The tune changed every time a car drove past.

In the orphanage, she would lie awake and stare at the walls. She remembered the small metal bed and how the springs had dug into her flesh through the thin mattress. Listening to some of the other girls cry themselves to sleep and hearing their sobs was strangely comforting. There, she wasn't the only one whimpering at night. Tonight she was alone.

The shadows taunted her with more painful memories.

The key scraped against the lock. Turning onto her side, she curled into the duvet and tucked up her legs into the foetal position. She closed her eyes and pretended to sleep. The same way she had when the house-mothers patrolled the hostels. The front door squeaked open. It took her a few seconds to realise that she was in her own flat and that she was safe. Her heart raced. She didn't want to fight anymore.

Louis closed the door softly behind him, bumped into something in the dark, and swore under his breath. His feet shuffled along the passage towards her then made their usual pit stop in the kitchen. The washing machine made a noise when it started. She heard the water from the shower. It was the same ritual every Sunday night. First he would visit his mother then he would come home. They would fight and he would disappear for a few hours, come back and put his uniform in the washing machine and then have a quick shower. Where had he been for the last four hours? Had he been with Janet? Or someone else?

She felt him slip into the bed and curl up behind her. His hair still wet. He wrapped his arms around her and kissed the nape of her neck.

"I'm sorry," he whispered into her hair.

"Me, too." Her voice was hoarse and sounded strange in the darkness.

His hands started to caress her breasts through her flannel pyjama shirt. He nibbled her earlobe and darted his tongue into her ear. She rolled over onto her back so that she could see his face, but could only make out the outline of his features.

Her index finger traced stubble from his chin to his mouth. He kissed her fingertip and then sucked it. She wanted to ask him where he had been and why he was being so affectionate. But asking him would ruin the moment and any chance of him making love to her would fly out of the window. Not being touched for another month was more than she could face. She ran her fingers through his hair and grabbed hold of the hair at the nape of his neck, pulling his face to hers. The smell of beer and cigarettes drifted up her nose. So that's what he'd been doing she thought. He'd probably been blowing off steam at Stix, the pool and billiards bar down the road.

His stubble scratched her skin but his kiss was tender. He teased her with his tongue while his hands explored her body. She had forgotten what it felt like to have his hands on her, in this way, affectionate, seeking, giving. He pulled her pyjama pants down, over her feet and threw them to the floor. While they made love, all she could think of was that whatever he had been doing in the last twenty-four hours, he should do it more often.

After he came inside her, he lay on top of her, breathing hard. She clung on to him with her arms and legs, staring at the ceiling. The sound of the wind outside mingled with the sound of Louis's breathing.

*

Tuesday, 2 July

Nico stood in a position that was starting to become a habit for him, in front of the pictures on the wall after the daily task team meeting on Tuesday morning. The incessant ringing of a phone on one of the desks exasperated him. He had been trying to get the women in the pictures to reveal something – anything – to him. He needed divine inspiration, maybe even a séance. He was stuck and only they knew the answers to the questions running around in his head. He finally answered the phone to shut it up.

"Van Staaden," he barked into the receiver, "Okay, give me fifteen minutes to get there." He slammed the phone down, dragged his wrinkled jacket off the back of a chair and jogged out of the room. Outside the task team operations room was a large open-plan office where policemen and women sat with telephones glued to their ears.

"Lucas, Koos, what are you two still doing here?" Nico shouted at them across the room. They tried to respond but the words didn't leave their open mouths in time. "Never mind giving me some excuse! Just call Dr. Papenfuss and that photographer, what's-his-face, and tell them to meet me in Silverton, corner of Pretoria and Republic. They've found another one," he shouted over his shoulder as he rushed out of the room.

*

A crowd had already formed outside the small rundown house in Silverton when Nico's car screeched to a halt. The same young constable from the previous Sunday's crime scene stood around and yet again looked bored. "Hey, you!" Nico shouted at him. "You're as useless as tits on a bull. Whenever I see you, you're standing around doing nothing. Make yourself useful, get some statements or find me a fucking witness and then get rid of the fucking crowd."

"Yes Captain. Sorry Captain." The young constable mumbled as he made his way towards the crowd of morbid spectators.

Nico stood waiting at the front door to the house. He took a drag of his cigarette and was writing down the name of the victim and all her relevant information when Pete and Thabiso arrived.

"Shocker of all shocks. The good Captain is actually on time for a change" said Thabiso, walking towards Nico.

"Oh, just shut up and take some photos of the crowd before I have them all arrested for loitering," Nico said, surprised by the anger in his own voice. The case was affecting him more than he wanted to admit. Thabiso looked from Nico to Pete, his mouth emulating a goldfish gasping for air.

"Didn't get it all this morning, huh?" Thabiso asked, trying to soften the atmosphere with some sarcasm.

"That's none of your fucking business. Just do your job," Nico said and crossed his arms. The banter only pissed him off even more.

"Fine, I'm going. Just remember you need me to be there when you're walking the scene." He picked up his camera and stalked off towards the crowd.

"Hey, what's up with you? You don't normally bite off people's heads for giving you grief," asked Pete.

"It's this case. It's starting to drive me crazy. If I don't catch him soon you'll have to lock me into one of those padded cells. I heard Weskoppies is quite nice this time of year."

"So have I, but I don't think they'll ever let you out again."

"How long do you think it'll take him to do the crowd shots?" Nico asked tilting his head in Thabiso's direction.

"A few minutes, maybe. How long does it normally take to snap a few shots?"

"At least I can finish my smoke in peace."

"Just don't forget to throw the stub in the correct bin."

"Oh, very funny. Are you always so cute this early in the morning?"

"Yes! Haven't you noticed?"

They watched Thabiso snap his last shot of the crowd and cars parked in the vicinity. He changed the zoom lens on the camera and put the previous one back in his black camera case. Nico watched as Thabiso looked around, checking to see if he had missed anything. Nico had to admit that the kid was good at his job. After checking he had shots from all angles Thabiso hung the camera around his neck and jogged back to Nico and Dr. Papenfuss, his camera bouncing up and down on his chest.

"Are you done?" Nico asked the slightly out-of-breath photographer, who looked as if he had just escaped from the front cover of Men's Health, which irked Nico even more.

"Yes," Thabiso answered and nodded his head.

The smell of rotting flesh was not as strong as it had been in the other victims' homes. The body was still relatively fresh. Nico led them through the dark house. The passage light didn't work. On closer examination, Nico discovered that the light bulb was encrusted with dust and had not been changed in months. The carpet was full of questionable stains. He heard a dog yelping in the backyard. That explained some of the stains. From the sound of its high-pitched yelping it was something small like a Maltese poodle, a rugby ball with legs. Every time he saw one of those little ankle-biters he wanted to kick them. Dogs were supposed to be big and have a deep bark. These chaff-chaff things were sent here to plague him, he was sure of it. It certainly hadn't been of any use to the victim.

In the kitchen, they found coffee which had been in the process of being made. The coffee mugs on the counter were chipped and in need of a scrub. The scene was similar to that at Theresa van Wyk's home and the other two victims. Thabiso took pictures from every angle of the room. Blood had coagulated on the dirty floor, which had probably not seen a mop in months. He would never be able to understand how people could live like this. The only reason Nico could think of was that she had given up all hope, if she'd ever had any to begin with.

In the second bedroom of this small, dismal house, they found all her dirty laundry piled up on a single bed with a foam mattress. The room smelt of wet dog. The material covering the mattress was worn through or ripped in places. Dog hair was all over the dirty laundry and all over the parts of the mattress that were visible.

In the lounge, magazines were strewn all over the floor.

They were predominantly *You* magazine. The furniture was in need of polish and the upholstery was old and worn. The springs were showing through the material. They walked into the main bedroom. The bed was unmade and clothes were strewn across the dirty floor. The smell of dirty laundry hung in the air. There was a thick layer of dust on her chest of drawers. Nothing in any of the rooms seemed to have been disturbed. They left the worst for last and made their way to the bathroom.

The bathroom light didn't work: there was an old paraffin lamp on top of the toilet cistern. The top of the lamp's glass chimney was pitch-black from use and lack of cleaning. The bathroom smelt of a strange mixture of urine and jasmine. The woman floating in the bath was bloated but still intact.

"She is Mrs. Erica Steenkamp, fifty-four years old, divorced and has a daughter she doesn't speak to. Or so the maid said." Nico said, reading from his notebook. "I still can't believe she had a maid," Nico said, looking around the filthy room and then back to his notes. "The neighbour found her. Apparently the dog was yapping all night and pissing off Mr Neighbour. So he came on over to complain and found the front door unlocked. He walked in, called her name a few times. Went through the house looking for Mrs. Steenkamp and found her in here. And like a good citizen, called us."

"Good thing Mr. Neighbour decided to yell at the victim instead of taking matters into his own hands and didn't just shoot or poison the mutt, which so many other people seem to be doing lately. She's still relatively fresh. Well, a lot more so than any of the other victims. We might actually get lucky and find something of value on this one. But I wouldn't hold my breath," Pete said and took out his notebook. "She fits the victim profile. Divorced, mid- to late-fifties, doesn't take care of herself or anything else. They were all down-and-out. I would say these women represent his mother. That's just a guess, mind you, but I would say that our boy definitely has issues with an older woman who played a major role in his life. He's also very controlled. I would say that this woman dominated him throughout his life and this is his sick way of taking back that control. He probably feels that she's castrated him." He looked up from the woman in the bath tub and looked at Nico. "Are you listening to me?"

"Oh *ja*, I heard you. His mother castrated him. Sorry, but I think I'm going to go back to the last crime scene. I keep thinking I've missed something," Nico said, staring down at yet another floating corpse.

6

The crime scene tape was still stretched across Theresa van Wyk's chipped front door. Nico ran his fingertips over the door and the tape. He gripped it and pulled it downwards. Taking the keys he'd borrowed from the caretaker out of his pocket, he unlocked the door, but paused inside the doorway. The smell of death still hung in the air. He had no idea what he was looking for, but hoped that he would find some small, overlooked, detail that would help him nail the murdering bastard.

The flat was dark, the curtains closed. Everything seemed to be the same as when he had left it on Sunday but it felt different. He had the distinct feeling that someone else had been there since the forensics team had vacated the premises: the sensation made his skin crawl. The powder from the fingerprinting was still visible on the yellowing light switches. Little black lines formed a web against the faded yellow backdrop. He walked into the lounge and swivelled around the room. His eyes swept over everything in sight. Nothing different. Nothing out of place. Nothing which could account for the feeling in the pit of his stomach.

He returned to the kitchen and stood in the doorway. His eyes travelled over the cupboards with dirty fingerprints on the handles. Over the door hanging at a slant. The one Theresa van Wyk had kicked in her struggle to live. Taking a Tums out of his jacket pocket, he opened the green and white packaging using his teeth and popped it into his mouth. The lemon flavour started to fizz as he chewed it.

The docket containing all the reports on Mrs. Van Wyk's murder, including the crime scene photograph album, was nestled under his arm. He went through the pictures and found those taken in the kitchen. He put the docket down on the counter. Thabiso hadn't missed a single inch of the room. He'd managed to capture all the horror that had taken place in this small kitchen. This had been the place where Theresa van Wyk had taken her last breath. He took another cursory look around the room and compared it with the photographs in front of him. There didn't seem to be anything missing. He picked up the docket and photo album and walked out of the kitchen and into the dark passage.

In the bathroom he sat on his haunches, bobbing up and down to his own haunted rhythm. With every breath he inhaled the unmistakeable smell of rotting flesh drifted up his nostrils. The rental agent would have a tough time finding a new tenant. He was tempted to open a window and stick his head out of it but he held the impulse in check, as well as the rising bile which irritated his stomach ulcer. He reached into his pocket again and took out another Tums, popped it in his mouth and chewed on it while he put the photographs of the bathroom on the floor in front of him. He rested his elbows on his knees, his hands dangled between his legs. Looking down at the photos and then at the room around him, always keeping in mind that every crime scene is three dimensional. He looked at the floor, the walls and lastly the ceiling but there was nothing different. It was still the same as it had been on Sunday, except the woman's corpse was missing. He put the bathroom photographs back into the docket, stood up, closed the shower curtain and walked back into the dark hallway. He took a few steps towards the front door when he remembered that he hadn't checked the bedroom. He turned around and walked back down the passage.

Her jacket was still crumpled up on the bed and the crucifix still hung on the wall. He took another look around the room, shrugged his shoulders and turned to leave.

But something wasn't right.

Something was missing.

He turned back and looked at the bedside table. He dumped the docket on the bed and paged through the album. He found the one he was looking for right at the back. Murphy's Law, he thought, whenever you're looking for something it's always right at the back. The silver-framed wedding photo, present in the pictures, was missing from next to the bed.

*

Natalie sat at a table in the back of the coffee shop across the road from the law firm where she worked. It was always full of attorneys and their clients at lunchtime. Janet was late, as usual. Lunch time traffic was a problem. It was an excuse she'd become comfortable making for Janet over the years. Natalie chewed the skin on the edge of her thumb as she waited for the waitress to notice that she was sitting there. She desperately needed some coffee. The caffeine would steady her frayed nerves.

It was a strange feeling wondering whether or not she could trust the two people she thought would never betray her. She'd always believed that the bond between her, Janet and Louis was unbreakable. Now she wasn't sure if she could trust either of them. They'd always been the two people she would trust with her life, her soul. They'd always protected each other. She'd never kept anything from them, but now it seemed they'd been keeping secrets. How many other things had they kept from her over the years?

How could the two people who'd gone to such lengths to protect her when they were teenagers, be so duplicitous? The memory was as fresh and sweet as though it had just happened. She could still see them sneaking into the orphanage that night after she'd confided in them. Louis took her place in the bed and waited for the old bastard to make his way down the passageway and into the room that she shared with five other girls. He'd ignored the others and slithered into her bed, where Louis waited with a knife. She and Janet were under the bed. The old man hadn't expected that. She hadn't heard what Louis said. She'd only heard the sound of her own heart beat. The old bastard never bothered her or any of the other girls after that.

She spotted Janet's blonde head as she walked into the restaurant and watched her look around the room. Janet's blue eyes roamed over the faces closest to her and then squinted to see towards the back. Janet really should wear her glasses out in public, Natalie thought; she, on the other hand had the eyes of a hawk. They even looked like hawks' eyes, or that was what Louis always told her. That was when he was in a good mood. When he was angry with her he said she had the eyes of a witch.

She stood up and waved so Janet could see her. Sitting down again, she waited for her friend to weave her way around the other tables. A waitress arrived at their table the moment Janet sat down; they ordered coffee. It irked Natalie that the waitress had ignored her the entire time she'd been waiting but decided to pay attention when Janet arrived. The little bitch wouldn't be getting a tip. Janet grabbed the menu and perused it with hungry eyes.

"So ..." Janet said over the menu. "Do you want to start or should I?"

"Well ..." Natalie looked down at her hands. She needed to stop chewing her fingernails she decided. "Since you called this little powwow, you can start."

"Thanks ..." she took a breath and blew it out slowly. "It's that fucking-bitch-ex-girlfriend of Nico's."

"What about her?"

"She keeps calling him at all times of the night."

"What on earth for? Does she want him back or something?"

"She claims she wants to talk to him about this case he's working on but I don't buy it. If that were it she would call him at work and not at home."

The waitress interrupted them before Natalie could say anything else. The tip of her shoe caught on the edge of a tile. She tripped, sending a cup of hot coffee flying. The hot black liquid landed in Natalie's lap. With a yelp of pain Natalie sprang out of her seat and grabbed the waitress.

"You fucking stupid cow," she screamed.

"I'm sorry, ma'am," the waitress stammered

"You've ruined my suit. How am I supposed to go back to work looking like this?"

"Nats, it's okay. It'll dry," Janet said, touching Natalie's shoulder. "You can let go of the waitress now."

Natalie let go of the frightened waitress, who ran straight

into the arms of a very unhappy-looking manager. The manager marched the waitress back to Natalie and Janet's table.

"I apologise for this accident, ladies," the manager said. His oversized moustache bristled. "Your lunch will be on the house."

"So does that mean I'll actually get to drink the coffee instead of having it poured all over me?" Natalie asked.

"Yes, ma'am. I'll bring you a fresh cup right away."

"Thank you and another waitress would be nice as well, one who actually knows what she's doing," Natalie said, as she sat down, clenching and unclenching her fists.

"So ... I don't suppose you could do that to Nico's ex?" Janet asked, a slight smile playing on her lips.

"Sorry. Went a little overboard there, didn't I?"

"Well maybe just a smidge. I mean, you did have the poor girl's hair in quite a grip."

"Did I? I didn't even notice." She looked down at her lap, hoping that her eye's wouldn't betray the absolute glee she'd felt at seeing that bitch waitress cower in fear. She felt the scalding heat on her legs. The pain was strangely exhilarating. She took a deep breath and exhaled slowly. "So where were we?" Natalie asked, fighting for control.

"Seriously, do you think you could do that to her?"

"Now you're the one overreacting. Nico loves you. You have nothing to worry about," Natalie said, not really being honest. "So who is this woman, anyway?'

"Helen Stratford."

"From the SABC News?"

"That's her."

"You're kidding?" Janet was screwed. Helen Stratford was gorgeous. Natalie couldn't help but wonder how Nico had managed to land her as a girlfriend, he wasn't exactly what she would have thought of as a stud. "Why did they break up?"

"Nico won't talk about it but from what I can gather, she was using him for leads on stories. He was working on an important murder case and because of her, the guy somehow managed to get away with it. Nico's boss blamed him for leaking it to the press or something like that."

"See? You have nothing to worry about. She screwed up and you haven't. Her loss."

"You're right. I'm just being silly." Janet took another breath and exhaled more slowly this time. "So, do you have any news?"

"Well …"

"Come on. I can see from your face that something's up."

"Something's certainly up," Natalie said with a smile. "Okay … well … you know Louis's little problem?" Natalie kept an eye on Janet's face for any tell-tale signs of betrayal.

"Yes. What about it?" Janet asked, not meeting Natalie's gaze.

"It looks like it might be clearing up."

"Really?" Honest surprise mixed with something Natalie couldn't interpret.

"We made love on Sunday and it was incredible. He did things I didn't even know he knew how to do. I think we may get through all the issues together after all." She felt a blush creep up from her neck to her cheeks. She'd always confided the most intimate details of her relationship with Louis to Janet, but telling her these things now felt a little uncomfortable.

"That's great. I'm so happy for you." Her voice, however, belied that sentiment. Natalie picked up on the insincerity in her voice. Had her best friend really stabbed her in the back in the worst possible way?

"Are you okay?"

Janet's voice startled her. She shook all the dark thoughts out of her mind.

"Sorry. I was just thinking about something I need to take care of," she said and smiled. "Now what do you want to eat?"

*

Nico took the stairs down to the first floor and knocked on

the caretaker's door. The caretaker was wearing the same blue shorts lodged under his voluminous belly. How could the bugger be wearing shorts in the middle of winter? The caretaker, who introduced himself as Koos, invited him in. His flat was not at all what Nico had been expecting. There weren't any oily engine parts lying on the carpet in the process of being repaired, or any rusty tools strewn across the dining room table. It was clean. There were fresh flowers on the table in a plain glass vase. Scatter cushions were arranged on the light beige sofa.

"My wife loves to clean; if I dump anything on the floor she picks it up within five seconds. I've actually timed her doing it," the caretaker said, as if reading Nico's mind. "Does your wife do funny things like that?" Koos asked.

"I'm not married. The reason I'm here, Mr …?"

"Just call me Koos, everybody else does."

"Okay, Koos. Has anybody been into Mrs van Wyk's place since Sunday?"

"I don't think so. This is a big block of flats. I don't see everybody's comings and goings you know."

"Yes, I realise that you can't be in more then one place at a time, sir, but did anyone ask you for a key to her flat or did you see anyone hanging around here in the last day or two?"

"Wait a minute. There was this one guy. Actually he was one of yours."

"One of mine?"

"*Ja*, a cop."

"What did he look like?"

"He looked like a cop. A young cop. You guys all look the same in uniform."

"I don't suppose you noticed what rank he was?"

"Sorry, I just saw the uniform. He said that some evidence had been left behind and that he needed to get it. I just opened up for him and waited outside while he went and got whatever it was that he needed."

Nico cursed silently.

"Did you see what he took?"

"Nah, sorry. I wasn't really looking, you know. I didn't want to get in his way."

He could quite happily have decked the idiot but he doubted that it would have made much difference to the man's face.

"So let me get this straight, a young policeman in uniform asked you to unlock her flat so he could remove something and you didn't get a good look at him and you didn't get his name? Is that about right?"

"Yes. Are you implying that I did something wrong? He was one of yours, for fuck's sakes. You don't argue with your types, that'll get you tossed into the choky."

"Thank you, sir, if you see him again please let me know," Nico said, handing him his business card. Then he turned and walked away. The caretaker stood in the doorway looking confused.

"Oh, one more thing ..." Nico said from the top of the stairs "Did you open the shower curtain when you found Mrs. van Wyk's body?"

"Um ... I ... I might have done. I can't really remember. Er ... I think I did. Why?"

"Oh, no reason. Thanks again and remember to let me know if you do spot that cop again," Nico shouted as he jogged down the stairs.

7

This was where he'd first seen Theresa van Wyk. She'd been drunk. The only time he'd seen her sober was the night she died. It was here in this small shopping centre's parking area that he decided it was time for her to die. Now it was time for him to find another one to take *that* Bitch's place in hell.

He watched people come and go. Some went into the small pizza shop or walked past him through the walkway to the Spar at the back. A young woman and a little girl walked out of the flower shop with a large bunch of mixed flowers. A wild array of colours, reds, yellows and blues blended together. That harpy never had flowers in her place. A weathered-looking man sold second-hand books outside the DVD shop. His brown knitted jersey should have found its way into the trash a few years ago. A middle-aged woman walked past his passenger-side door and almost fell onto the bonnet of his patrol car in her hurry to get to the bottle store. He watched her as she stumbled through the door. He sat there watching, waiting for another five minutes.

The woman came out of the bottle store carrying a black plastic packet with the neck of a bottle of Vodka sticking out. She walked past him once again and tripped, landing on her knees and hands on the tar behind his rear left bumper. He got out, walked over to her and helped her back onto her feet.

"Are you all right?" he asked her, once she was tottering on her feet.

"Yes. I'm fine and so's the bottle. Now get your bloody hands off me." Her speech was slurred and the smell of cheap booze drifted from her mouth.

She pushed him away and stumbled across the parking area. Drivers hooted and swerved to avoid hitting her. She managed to cross Anna Wilson Street without being knocked down andbuzzed herself through the green gate of her block of flats.

"I'll see you soon," he mumbled to himself, got back into his patrol car and drove out of the parking area.

*

The room was dark. The candles, which Janet insisted on lighting whenever she came over, gave the room a softness absent during the day. The street lights and the flickering candle flames danced on the walls. Janet's head rested on Nico's lap while his fingers played with her hair. His thoughts kept returning to the missing silver frame and the bathroom curtain. Why did the Strangler close the curtain after he killed them? Nico tilted his head back against his old leather couch and tried to concentrate on the movie Janet wanted him to watch with her. It was some romantic movie with Julia Roberts. He got a glance of Julia Roberts's wild red hair from under his eyelashes. She was getting old. He closed his eyes and heard Julia Roberts laughing. Her laughter turned into the Strangler's laughter. Yep, he thought, the murdering piece of shit was probably sitting at home laughing at him because he had no idea who the killer was. But he was getting closer.

"So laugh as much as you want you bastard. I'm going to get you," he whispered.

"What did you say?" Janet was sitting up and looking at him.

"Hmm ... what?" he asked.

"You were mumbling something about 'going to get you'."

"Oh ... was I? I didn't realise I'd said that out loud."

"Are you okay?"

"I'm fine. Aren't you supposed to be watching old Julia over there? She's much better looking than I am."

"I'm not exactly into women and as attractive as she may be, I much prefer looking at you." Wrapping her arms around his neck, she kissed him. "So? Do you want to talk about it or are you just going to mumble to yourself all night?"

"It's this case. It's driving me nuts. That's all. But I'm sure Julia Roberts is far more interesting."

"You're not getting off the hook that easily. So spill it."

"Are you sure you want to hear about it?"

"Abso-bloody-lutely."

"Okay, you win," he said and took a breath, giving him

time to consider what and how much he could tell her. "This guy is one sick puppy and it's starting to look like the Doc's profile was right about it being a cop."

"Why are you so sure it's a cop and why does it have to be a guy? Why can't it be a woman?" She frowned. He loved it when she frowned like that.

"Well, for one thing the killer has to be incredibly strong and I don't know about you but I don't know any women who are that butch. Plus when women kill, it's not usually the way they do it. Women tend to shoot or use poison. A male wearing what could have been a police uniform was seen leaving the first victims flat. I also went back to all the murder scenes and, at each and every single one of them, the caretaker or neighbour told me a cop had been back to the scene after we had cleared it. A man: not a woman. The cop told them evidence had been left behind. So of course they didn't think twice about letting him back in to retrieve it. At each scene he took something both personal and had a small cash value. But there's something else that's bugging me."

"What's that?"

"I think he feels sorry or regrets his actions or something like that, afterwards."

"Why do you say that?"

"After he's killed them and posed them in the bathtub, he closes the shower curtain. Pete tells me if a rapist, for example, puts his victim's skirt back down and covers her privates, that he feels remorse. Whereas a rapist who leaves his victim's privates open for the world to see feels absolutely nothing about what he's done."

"Oh, okay. Pete probably knows what he's talking about."

"Yes, he does. It took him long enough to get his doctorate in psychology. Anyway, where was I?" he asked, rubbing the bridge of his nose between his thumb and index finger. "Oh, *ja* ... our killer, he closes the curtain on his deed. So he still has a bit of humanity left in him and hopefully that little bit of humanity will get him caught. Or maybe, if I'm lucky, he'll get stupid."

"Interesting, but do you know what?"

"No, what?"

"You think about this guy way too much and I know just the way to get him out of your head, for a while anyway."

"Oh really, and how do you intend to do that?"

"Mmmm. Wouldn't you like to know?" she said as she unzipped his pants.

"Are you sure you want to do this?"

"Oh yes."

She stuck her hand inside his underpants and took a firm hold of him. Her fingers were magical tentacles, touching, stroking, making him feel things he hadn't felt since Helen. He felt himself respond to her touch. She looked up at him with a pleased grin. He took her glasses off their perch on her nose and kissed her.

"What happened to wanting to wait?"

"We've waited long enough."

She bent her head down, freed him from his jeans which were getting tighter and licked the tip of his penis.

"Oh, god," he murmured

She started sucking.

"Oh, God. You're incredible."

"You like that do you?" she said, looking up at him.

He pulled her head up to him and kissed her hard. Picking her up, he carried her down the passageway to his bedroom. It was the first time he'd had a woman in his bed in a very long time. He just hoped he'd live up to her expectations and his own.

*

"Okay boys and girls, settle down," Nico said, looking at his team. He focused on each of them, finding it difficult to believe any one of them might be the man he was after. He had worked with each of them for years. He knew them all, had gone out drinking with them, *braaied* with them and their families. Pete's profile had to be wrong. He had to be wrong. The caretaker and the other witnesses had to be wrong.

"Dr. Papenfuss has amended and improved the profile on the Bathroom Strangler. According to him our boy has a mother fixation. In other words, for those of you who don't speak psyche, he wants to kill his mother. He probably also killed or maimed animals when he was a kid. The fact that he kills on Sundays has to have something to do with his mother. You know, the whole thing about Sundays being a family day and all of that crap. Also, statistically speaking, people are more prone to commit suicide on Sundays. Our boy decided homicide was a much healthier way of expressing himself. And considering he kills every Sunday, we only have a couple of days to go till the next one drops. So people, we need to get a move on. Has anyone found out anything about the piano wire that our boy uses?" Nico waited for a response. His audience looked at the floor, at the wall, everywhere except where he wanted them to look. They avoided looking at him.

"So I take it that's a 'no'. Would one of you wonderful people please tell me why the fuck not?"

Silence. Someone in the back of the room coughed.

"Eben," he shouted across the room at the man guilty of coughing. "Would you be so kind as to tell me why nobody here is able to tell me the reason why the forensic team's hard work has not been able to bear fruit?"

"Because it's a dead end," Eben mumbled

"What was that Eben? Please speak up. We can't hear you."

"I said it's a dead end. Manufacturers aren't able to tell us what kind of piano it comes from because it's the same kind of wire that they use for every single type of piano that's sold in this country. Do you have any idea how many pianos there are in this country? There are a shitload, okay? So short of doing a house-to-house search of everyone in Pretoria and asking them if they have a piano with a missing E sharp or F wire, we have jack-shit. Okay?"

"Okay. Thank you Eben, but that sounds like a fucking cop-out and I think you should check again. While you're at it you can check sales records for names of people who have bought that type of wire, also have a look at piano tuners who have had to replace that wire for any of their clients. No wonder the people out there think we're useless. We can't even find out about a piece of wire. The death toll is up to five. People are scared, so watch yourselves out there. Kindly get your arses in gear and catch the mother-hating bastard. Thank you and get out."

He watched them file out of the room. When they found the next body he would be ready and waiting. He realised that he would have to carry out his plan alone. Not knowing who he could trust was a royal pain in the arse.

*

<u>Sunday, 7 July</u>

She closed one eye trying to coerce the three dotted lines to become one. That didn't work. She decided to aim her car at the middle line and straddled it. White flashing lights winked at her in the rearview mirror. . It took her a few moments and a disembodied voice telling her to pull over before she realised that the cops were trying to get her attention. Usually the cops flashed blue lights at her and their sirens gave her a headache. She far preferred this new way of doing it, it was less noisy.

"Shit," she slurred, as her fuzzy mind grasped that she could be arrested again. She hid the empty bottle of vodka under her seat with shaky hands. The policeman got out of his car and slammed his door. The sound of the slamming door ricocheted around her head a few times.

She put her hands in front of her eyes trying to protect them from the bright torch light the policeman insisted on shining in her face.

"Have you been drinking, Ma'am?" a deep voice asked her.

"No, ossifer. I never drink on the Lord's Day," she said,

trying not to slur her words. She sounded like a weedeater, inadvertently placing z's in all the wrong places.

"I see, ma'am. Do you normally drive in the middle of the road?" he asked her.

"Yes, osfizer, I always drive in the middle of the road. I prefer to drive that way. It makes things so much more interesting."

"I see, ma'am. I should actually take you down to the station for driving under the influence, but the holding cells are usually full on a Sunday night. So I think I'll drive behind you and make sure you get home safely."

"Thank you, Ossifer, but I'm fine. You don't need to worry about me. I'll get home just fine."

"I'd rather make sure you get home in one piece, ma'am. I'll sleep better tonight"

"Suit yourself, but I live just around the corner. I can make it there on my own."

"I know, ma'am, but I'll feel better knowing you got home safe and sound."

"I live just over there," she said, waving her hand in the general direction of where she lived."

"Okay, ma'am, I'll be right behind you."

The bright light disappeared and she heard the footsteps retreating. A car door slammed shut, making her cringe. It took her a few engine-grinding tries before she managed to put the gear lever into first. She straddled the dotted white line and drove at 20km/h. The steering wheel decided to go its own way once or twice and she bounced on and off the pavement. She veered right into Anna Wilson Street, bumped onto the pavement and screeched to a halt outside the green fence of her block. The complex was three different blocks of flats, each three storeys high.

She climbed out of her car on unsteady legs. He caught her when she stumbled and helped her to her feet. She fumbled through her oversized handbag for the remote control for the gate. She hated that remote. It was never where she'd put it. It always hid from her. Her trembling fingers found the remote. She dropped it. He picked it up. The gate wheels squeaked on their tracks as they opened. She stumbled once again and fell to her knees. She tasted vodka and bile. Her non-existent stomach muscles tensed as she heaved. Her mouth opened: it felt as though her jaw would dislocate as the hot liquid poured out of her open mouth onto the pavement.

She felt his strong hands grip her around her waist and help her to her feet once again. He half-carried her through the open gate, leaving her car on the pavement. She didn't remember locking the car door. He pushed open the wooden door to the second block and helped her inside. She tasted bile and heaved. They made it to the pot plant in the entrance hall just in time.

"Oh well," he said. "The plant won't need any other nutri-ents for a while."

He propped her up against the wall and waited for the lift to take them to the third floor.

The lift rattled all the way up. On several occasions she thought she would lose what was left of her stomach. Her jaw hurt and her throat burned. She felt like she was dying. Never again, she swore, would she do this to herself. A whole bottle of vodka in one sitting was not a good idea. If she didn't die of alcohol poisoning tonight, she promised herself she would never touch the stuff ever again. She just had to get through tonight.

She felt the lift come to a jolting stop, which sent what was left of her stomach up her throat. His hands gripped her fleshy arms and she was moving once again.

"What number?" he asked.

"Number thirteen." She heard a strange voice reply. The voice sounded like hers, but she couldn't be sure. The bile rose again but she managed to swallow it. It tasted of acid and vodka.

"Almost there," he said. "Just keep it in for a little bit longer."

She felt the brick wall beneath her fingers as he leaned her against the wall at her front door. She heard the bell-like jingle of keys. She floated and then hit the floor with a thump. He left her on the floor while he fiddled with the keys, trying to find the right one for her front door. Her shoes, which were too big for her, slipped off her feet. The door creaked open. She felt his strong hands grab her and pick her up again.

The familiar smell of home wafted up her nostrils. She felt her carpet beneath her feet and wondered what had happened to her shoes. He let go of her and she found herself once again on her hands and knees.

"Where's your bathroom?" he asked her, his voice was distant and she had trouble deciding where it was coming from.

"Down the passage. Somewhere over there." She flailed her right arm about, pointing to the left. She started to gag and heave. She was sure there wasn't anything left in her stomach to throw up. She started to crawl down the dark, narrow passage towards her bathroom. Muffled footsteps followed her and she tried to crawl faster. The footsteps still followed her. The tiled floor was cold on her naked knees. She felt her way in the dark towards the toilet. The tiles felt gritty beneath her fingertips. The base of the toilet was wet and sticky. The smell of stale urine wafted up her nostrils and she couldn't hold it any longer. She managed to lift the toilet seat in time for the rest of her stomach to leave her body. The light had been switched on and she wondered how that had happened.

She rested her head on the toilet seat and waited patiently for the next wave to hit her. The room turned slowly. Putting her hand flat on the floor, she tried to stop it from spinning out of control. She felt the man's presence behind her and closed her eyes. The toilet seat felt cold against her hot cheek. It was strangely comforting.

A shadow passed over her and she opened her left eye a fraction. He loomed over her and was fuzzy around the edges. She tried to focus but gave up and closed her eye again. Something rough and sharp bit into her throat. She couldn't breathe. She tried to get a grip on it and pull it away. It pulled tighter. She tried to stand up but felt something push her back.

"Breathe, I need to breathe." She tried to suck in some air. It never made it to her lungs. She had nothing left inside her. She let go and slipped away.

8

Nico took the call on Tuesday morning. The latest victim had been found. It was now time to put his plan into action. The inactivity and the helplessness of it all drove him crazy. But another death brought him closer to catching the bastard. Relief that there was another body bothered his conscience but the new body was necessary to his plan. He exhaled, grabbed his wrinkled jacket and walked out of the noisy police station, climbing into an unmarked white Nissan Almera.

The police radio buzzed with activity. A robbery was in progress in Sunnyside, also commonly referred to as Scumyside. Shots had been fired and an officer was in pursuit of the suspects.

"Well, that's nothing new," he mumbled to himself.

Driving down Church Street, the morning traffic was moving in the other direction towards the heart of Pretoria. Most of them were probably government employees on the gravy train. Prostitutes stood on the street corners in mini skirts that could pass for belts. Beggars stood at traffic lights, in the middle of the road, brandishing cardboard signs, each one of them looking more sorrowful than the next. The irony was that they probably made more than he did. He had to laugh when he spotted a young white man brandishing a sign claiming to have a three mistresses and a thirst to support. That earned the beggar a five rand coin.

He drove past the Union Buildings and the Sheraton Hotel. He would never understand why they put a five-star hotel so close to Sunnyside. Just one road down and you were in crime central. The only thing the hotel had in its favour was the view of the Union Buildings. He always marvelled at the sight of one of the country's most majestic Government buildings. It was one of the few buildings that made him proud to be a South African. People often took their afternoon siesta on the lawns in front of the building, which had caused a lot of controversy during the height of the Apartheid era. In the mid eighties the international press had reported that the men and women sleeping in the sun were actually dead bodies that had been left to rot.

He drove through Hatfield and turned left at the driving range and drove towards Queenswood. At the Kilnerpark Spar he turned right into Lynette Street. He climbed onto the curb outside the green gate of the latest victim's block of flats. Police cars were parked on either side of the narrow street. The all too familiar scene of blue lights flashing made his stomach pitch and yaw. He felt as though he were standing on the deck of a ship during a turbulent storm. Nervous excitement filled him.

Once on the third floor he found his way to number thirteen. The barrier tape marked the scene in much the same way the flashing blue lights outside notified everyone in the neighbourhood that a crime had been committed. He looked around. The scene was an exact replica of all the others. They were all interchangeable. Thabiso was snapping away with his camera. Pete leaned against the wall having a smoke and waited for him. He felt as though he was experiencing *déjà vu*. He experienced it a lot these days.

"I hope they've already dusted for prints," Nico said to Pete when he reached him.

"Would you relax? Of course they have. I'm not a complete moron and besides it's a pigsty in there, a little ash won't make much difference."

"As long as you don't contaminate the scene I don't really give a shit. Just remember to throw the *stompie* in the right bin," he said as he went inside.

The scene in the bathroom differed from all the previous murder scenes in that there was vomit in the toilet basin and blood on the seat. Unlike the other victims she had been killed in the bathroom and not in the kitchen. He made a mental note to remind the forensics guys to take samples to be analysed in the lab.

He truly believed that a large percentage of catching criminals was just plain dumb luck. He wished he could say all the bad guys he had put behind bars were there because he was a genius. The sad truth was that the criminals had made stupid mistakes. This killer, on the other hand, hadn't yet. But he would, eventually, and Nico would be there. Waiting.

The victim was Tanya McKenzie. According to her neighbours she was a notorious drunk. Her husband had left her for his secretary a few years ago and left her with just the clothes on her back, quite literally. She had found a friend in a bottle of vodka. Her neighbours had seen her leave late on Sunday evening, probably going on one of her usual binges. It was normal to see her stumble to her car with a bottle in hand and then take off, leaving most of her tyres behind. The rumour was that she went and harassed her ex-husband and his new young wife. No one bothered to stop her. One of the neighbours had tried the first time she had done it, but had been smacked over the head with her bottle of vodka and had his skull cracked for his trouble. No one had tried since and no one had seen her come home that night. Her car had been found outside the complex the next morning. A constable had found an empty bottle of vodka wedged under the driver's seat.

He went down to the ground floor and had a look at her car. It was a battered old Ford held together by the rust marks. The tow truck driver was manoeuvring it onto the back of the truck. He watched the tow truck drive off and thought about her last few hours on this earth. In her drunken state she must have been an easy target. This inebriated condition made a thought buzz in his mind. There was something bothering him about the murders, something he had missed. It was like an itch in one of those hard-to-reach places. He wanted to scratch it but could never quite find it. All the murder scenes flashed through his mind. He thought about the empty vodka bottle in Tanya McKenzie's car and the brandy bottle in Theresa van Wyk's dustbin. He realised this was the connection between all the victims. They were all drunks. Well, they were according to their neighbours. He smacked his palm to his forehead.

"Idiot," he admonished himself. "Why didn't I see it before?"

He turned around and walked back towards the building when he spotted Pete walking out of the glass door towards him. An idea started to take shape in his mind.

"Howzit, Doc," he said, once the doctor was within hearing distance. "I have a little theory I need your help with."

"Okay, what do you want now?" the doctor asked.

"Would you call the Government lab for me?"

"Why? Don't you remember how to use a phone any more or do I look like a fucking secretary to you?"

"Ummm, come to think of it I can definitely see you in a tight skirt and heels," he said grinning. "But seriously, would you do this as a favour? I have a shitload of stuff to take care of and it's just one little phone call."

"Fine – on condition that you stop picturing me in a skirt."

"Consider it done. I need you to ask them to check the blood work from all the victims. The lazy bastards haven't come back to me about any of them."

"Have you forgotten about the backlog at the lab?"

"I keep hoping for a miracle and that the lab would just once be able to get me the results when I need them, without screwing them up or taking years to do them. Is that really asking too much?"

"I think you may be asking a bit much, but is there anything specific you want the guys at the lab to look for?"

"*Ja*, I want to know what the alcohol level was in all their blood streams."

"Come to think of it, that's a good idea. It'll certainly confirm my suspicion that he targets drunken women. And then I think we should issue a press release and let them know the victim profile." Nico frowned. "Look, I know how you feel about issuing the details but we have a responsibility to let women of a certain age know that they need to be aware of the goings on around them."

"Fine, but we need to be careful about the wording. I don't

want a full-scale panic from all the alcoholic old women out there. We have enough crank calls on our hands as it is."

"I'll word it very carefully. I promise."

"You'd better and don't forget to call me once you get the results from the lab."

Nico, still frowning, walked back towards the building leaving Pete very pleased with himself for persuading Nico to agree to release some information to the press. But he wasn't all that sure how Colonel Moses Molwedi would feel about it. The big man might not be all that thrilled with Pete's idea or Nico's consent, especially after the whole Helen debacle.

*

Nico waited for everyone to leave the scene. He watched the forensics' van drive around the corner and disappear down Lynette Street. He parked his car in the parking lot across the street and made sure he had a perfect view of the entrance to the block of flats. Fortunately there was only one entrance to keep an eye on. This was probably where the killer had waited and watched. He wondered what the killer had done to pass the time while he stalked his victim. Had he listened to Radio Jacaranda or 5FM? Did he drink coffee or tea or a beer?

The winter morning sun rose higher in the sky. It began to get hot in the car and the damn thing didn't have aircon. He switched on the car radio. Some woman was reading the news on Radio Jacaranda. She gave an update on the Bathroom Strangler case, letting the general populace know that there'd been another victim. Kurt Darren took over and a local Afrikaans singer he'd never heard of before and whom he hoped he'd never hear again, moaned through the speakers as his cell phone started ringing in his jacket. The speakers in the back of the car objected to the interference caused by the incoming call. He turned down the volume and answered it.

"Hi, Doc. What have you got for me?"

"They all had alcohol content in their blood streams except Theresa van Wyk. She was the only sober one at the time of death."

"Why the fuck wasn't the blood tested before? What's the point of taking a sample from the victims if they aren't going to test it?"

"Nico, I'm sorry. The lab is snowed under and besides, didn't we have this conversation just a short while ago?"

"I don't care if we have this conversation a hundred fucking times."

"Hey, don't shoot the messenger. You can vent with the guys over at the lab as much as you like. Don't take your shit out on me."

Nico could hear him sulking through the phone.

"Look, I'm sorry. I'm just frustrated."

"You aren't the only one. Don't you think I want to catch this guy as badly as you do?" Pete took a breath. "I know this brings back memories of what happened to your mother but you have to realise that you aren't alone in this."

"Please, don't pull your head-shrink stuff on me."

"Nico, you need help."

"Okay Doc, I'll promise to get help after the case is over if you promise to leave my mother out of this."

"Fine, but when this is over I'm going to check you into therapy myself."

"Okay, Doc. Whatever you say, but can we please get off my problems and back to the case."

"Sorry. Now where were we?" Pete asked.

"The fact is that if I'd had those test results, I could have made the connection between the victims earlier."

"That they were all drunk the night they died?"

"Yes, well all of them except Theresa van Wyk."

"But she was also a heavy drinker according to her neighbours. So the connection still stands. They were all full-blown alcoholics."

"Another lead to follow up. I'll have someone check out the liquor stores in their neighbourhoods. Maybe somebody saw someone watching the victims. He has to find them somewhere; maybe he uses the bottle stores to find his victims. It's one of the best places to find an alcoholic."

"Good idea and at least it'll keep you busy and out of trouble." His voice faded and Nico could hear someone else in the background. The doctor's voice came back. "Sorry, Nico, but I have to go. I've got to check on something for another murder case." The line went dead. Another piece in the puzzle found but he didn't know where it fitted.

He needed the toilet. One of the many drawbacks of doing a stake-out alone was the difficulty of taking a leak when needed. Maybe he should have asked one of the women at the station to back him up. None of them would have had the strength to garrotte someone and therefore couldn't be included as suspects. Come to think of it maybe one or two of them could: Mavis was a big girl and he wouldn't want to meet her in a dark alley. But if things became dangerous he would rather be alone than have an inexperienced woman guarding his back. If Janet had any clue how he felt about women in the police force she would have his balls in a sling. His bladder started to pull. Maybe he should have trusted Pete. The doctor was a good guy and if he trusted Pete he wouldn't have to sit here trying to control his bladder. He shouldn't have had that last cup of coffee this morning and, to make things worse, he was thirsty.

Think of the desert, he kept telling himself, don't think of water. Whatever you do, don't think about water. Except trying to tell himself not to think about water and needing to empty his bladder only made him more desperate for the toilet.

He opened the glove compartment and found an empty 500ml Valpré bottle. Someone had probably left it behind on a previous stake-out. It must have been missed during the car's weekly clean out. Nico didn't really care where the bottle came from: all he cared about was that he could urinate in it. He unzipped his pants. The urine hitting the inside of the empty bottle was the most heavenly sound Nico had heard all day. Relief flooded over him. If he trusted Pete, he wouldn't have to piss in a bottle.

The Afrikaans singer was, thankfully, replaced by the Red Hot Chili Peppers, who were in turn replaced by Nickleback. He drummed his fingertips on the steering wheel in time with the music. Time ticked past and the radio's appeal started to wear thin. He just wanted the killer to hurry up and make his appearance. He watched a police car drive past slowly. He gripped the steering wheel and wondered if this was it, but the car kept on driving. He sat back in the seat and prepared himself for another long wait. The wind started to pick up. Red and brown leaves danced across the parking lot. Sheryl Crow was crooning something about soaking up the sun, when the police car returned.

He watched the police car drive past again slowly and do a U-turn at the corner. His heart pounded. The police car, a white Citi Golf with the usual police insignia on the door and blue stripe, pulled up onto the curb. A young man in the standard dark blue police uniform with black Magnum boots got out of the car. He was too far away for Nico to make out his rank. He also managed to keep his back to Nico, so he couldn't see the man's face. Nico waited for the cop to go through the pedestrian gate before getting out of his car and followed him. Nico stopped at the white Citi Golf with the intention of taking down the number but the licence plate had been removed.

"Shit," he said under his breath, scratched the back of his head, and looked in the direction the suspect had gone. He picked up his feet and ran or rather jogged in the same direction.

He pressed the button for the lift. It took too long to arrive and he decided to take the stairs up to the third floor instead. He took them two at a time and was breathing heavily when his right foot touched the landing. He bent over to catch his breath and turned his head in the direction of number thirteen, in time to glimpse a blond head popping out of the door of Tanya McKenzie's flat.

"Hey, you!" he shouted as he power-walked towards his suspect.

The man didn't miss a beat. He turned in the opposite direction and ran down the passage towards the fire escape.

"Damn! Why do they always have to run?" he grumbled as he ran after him.

Nico chased him along the passage and down the stairs. His breath came in gasps. His suspect was fast and unfortunately in a lot better shape then he was. The suspect took the stairs three at a time and jumped the last four to the landing on each floor. Nico tried to do the same but managed to trip on the ground floor and sprawled, face first, on the ground where he landed. Tyres squealed. Nico raised his face from the ground to see the white police Citi Golf screech its way down the road.

"For fuck's sake! You fucking bastard!" he shouted as he got back on his feet. He kicked the air in frustration and wished he could be kicking the suspect's arse. He wasn't sure who he wanted to kick more, the suspect or himself. He bent over and put his head between his legs to quieten his laboured breathing.

"I really need to join a gym," he mumbled as he made his way back to his car. As he walked he dusted himself off. His grey slacks were now a dusty brown all the way down the front and his once-white shirt, where it wasn't a muddy brown, was soaking wet.

"Oh, well," he thought, "at least now I can take a proper leak that doesn't involve a bottle."

*

"You look like hell." It was the first thing Nico heard when entering the noisy charge office of the Pretoria Central police station. Builders in blue overalls were busy building concrete benches in the entrance and the smell of cement mingled with that of sweat, urine and blood. Startled by the closeness of the voice, Nico looked to his left to discover a bored-looking Louis leaning against the wall. There was something about the way he was leaning that struck Nico: it was catlike and stealthy, almost as if he was ready to pounce. He realised that everything about Louis could be described in that one phrase. The way he moved, the way he spoke, every action he made was feline and predatory.

"What are you doing here?" Nico asked him, struggling

to make himself heard above the voices of people waiting to report a crime.

"I caught this idiot trying to boost a car with a flat battery," he said, crooking his thumb over his shoulder at a dejected-looking boy, not more than thirteen, sitting on his haunches in the corner, staring at the handcuffs binding his wrists, "but as you can see the system's a bit busy today." He raised his eyebrows and tilted his head in the direction of the lines of people waiting their turn.

"It always is but it gets there eventually. It grinds slowly but finely," Nico said and looked at the boy in tattered jeans and muddy jersey. "He's just a scared kid."

The boy had street child stamped all over him: probably addicted to smoking glue. He wouldn't survive much longer on the streets. Nico had seen so many of them slip through the cracks and found their bodies in the mortuary.

"Okay. Then I'll let the little shit go." Louis turned around and unlocked the handcuffs. He dragged the boy to his feet by his left arm.

"Go on, scram," he said, as he kicked the boy's arse, "get out of here and don't get caught again."

The boy looked at him with a look of total and utter shock. A smile then broke out across his emaciated face, lighting it up. He turned tail and ran through the door.

"Why did you do that?" Nico asked, with as much shock on his face as the boy's.

"I thought that's what you wanted."

"What I wanted?"

"*Ja!* What was all that 'he's just a poor kid' stuff?"

"It was an observation, not an instruction to let him go."

"Oh."

"What do you mean 'Oh'?"

"So the kid gets a few more days of freedom, big deal. He'll be back."

"That's the problem ... *ag* ... forget it."

"Already forgotten. Now that that's out of the way, what happened to you, or shouldn't I ask?"

"I tripped and ate some pavement."

"Sounds painful. I was going to ask if you wanted to join me for a beer but I don't know if I want to be seen with you in public, looking like that."

"The beer sounds good and it'll wash the pavement taste out of my mouth but I don't know if I want to be seen with a guy in a rent-a-cop uniform."

"Are you mocking the uniform?"

"Me? Mock the uniform? Never!"

"So ... Tell me the truth, were you stuck in a dumpster all morning or something?"

"No, I'm just way too old and too fat to be chasing some guy who is probably ten years younger than I am."

"So you thought you could still keep up with the young studs of today's criminal association?"

"Yes."

"And ended up with your face in the dirt – very clever."

"Thank you! What can I say? I do try."

"I think you deserve that beer for the attempt."

"I don't think I deserve it; I might need it, but I don't deserve it."

"Okay, so the fucker got away from you. You'll get him next time."

"*Ja*. Next time," Nico sighed and dropped his head. He felt drained and angry with himself. Because of him another woman would be dead in a few days.

"Hey, snap out of it, bro. Tomorrow's another day and things will look a whole lot better after a few beers."

"I'm just going to put on another shirt."

"Let me guess ... you keep an extra shirt in the top drawer of your desk?"

"Wrong, it's in my bottom draw. You never know when you're going to get covered in blood and shit on this job."

"I'm glad I don't have to do your laundry. Now hurry up and change your shirt. There's a Black Label calling my name."

Nico walked through the crowded charge office and into the office he shared with two Lieutenant Colonels from the Detectives division, Steven Maritz and Paul Lubbe. Steven, also known as Laurel, was tall and skinny whereas Paul, known as Hardy, was short and squat. Luckily they were off somewhere else so he had his office all to himself for a change. They were only his superiors in rank, not in intellect. His desk was in the corner, opposite the window looking into the charge office. The office was a fishbowl. He closed the blinds on all windows, so that neither insiders nor outsiders could see him. Opening his bottom drawer, he removed a plain, light blue, button-down shirt. He shook it out and examined it: wrinkled and frayed at the cuffs but at least it was clean. He took off his favourite jacket and hung it on the back of his desk chair. It was navy blue. Janet had bought it in April for his birthday, the first present she'd bought him. He unbuttoned the dirty white shirt he was wearing. He sniffed it and crinkled up his nose. He needed some deodorant as well but that would have to wait till he got home. He took off the shirt, crumpled it up and tossed it into the open bottom drawer, then kicked the drawer closed. Nico buttoned up the last button of his shirt and was tucking it in over his white vest when Louis walked in and surveyed the room.

"Nice view," Louis said, moving the blind out of his way, peering through the gap to watch the comings and goings in the charge office.

"It has its moments," Nico said, buckling his belt.

"So is this where you guys get together to hunt down that killer."

"No, this is just my little fishbowl. The task team uses a boardroom upstairs. We converted it to look like a classroom. It suits our needs and we've given some of the clerical staff a few extra duties like answering crank calls."

"And I bet they just love you for it."

"Absolutely."

"So … can I see it?"

"See what?"

"The operations room?"

"I'm sorry, but the ops room is of limits to civilians."

"Come on. Can't you make an exception, just this once?"

There was something in the way he asked, the way he

pleaded to see the room that made Nico wonder about his motives, it made those bells clang in his head. Maybe seeing Louis' reaction to the photos on the walls would answer a few questions he had about him.

"Okay, I'll let you see it, but it's our little secret ."

"Excellent." Louis looked like an excited school boy who'd been granted access into an exclusive club.

Nico led him through the charge office towards the back of the police station. They walked up the dirty stairs in silence. The staircase smelt of urine and other body fluids that Nico didn't even want to think about. The station was not one of the cleanest in the city. He couldn't fathom why people used the stairs to take a piss when there were perfectly good toilets just down the passage. He only hoped that it wasn't his fellow policemen using the stairs as a toilet. The task team's operations room was on the first floor.

Nico led Louis along a narrow passage. Instead of plastering the walls in the station, they had simply painted over the brick, alternating between white and institutional-blue panels of paint. It was the same blue as the hanging files in his filing cabinet. There were dirty scuff marks all over the walls. Nico often felt that walking along these passages on his way to the operations room was, in a strange way, preparation for the grim task of facing the dead women whose pictures were stuck on the walls with Prestik.

The open-plan office outside was its usual hive of activity. The phones never stopped ringing. Young constables, fresh out of Police College, and the station's clerical staff were assigned to answer the crank calls. Serial killers always managed to bring all the psychos out of the woodwork, wanting their piece of the action. He'd even had a few people claiming to be the Bathroom Strangler. Thank heavens he and Pete had kept some facts of the case out of the press. It was, as far as he was concerned, the best way of determining which were crank calls and which were legitimate.

The door to the operations room was made of thin pressed wood. It was the kind of door that if given a good solid kick, it would splinter and the offending foot would go right through it. Nico opened the door and Louis pushed past him. The room was deserted. Only the victims' ghosts were here. Nico watched Louis's facial expressions change from curiosity to shock, then to what should have been horror but looked more like discomfort as he moved closer to the pictures. He couldn't help but wonder what Louis thought as he examined each of the victims. There was something in the way his eyes seemed to devour the images. It wasn't the reaction he'd expected. But everybody reacted differently to the grisly images on display.

The pictures reminded Nico of his failure that morning. He would be adding another set of photos to the grotesque collage when another body was discovered. He turned around and walked out of the room leaving Louis to stare at the dead women. He, on the other hand, couldn't face them. He leaned against the wall and waited for Louis to finish his morbid viewing.

A door, two doors down from the operations room, opened.

"Van Staaden, get in here." Colonel Moses Molwedi, Nico's boss, stood in the doorway and waited for Nico to enter his office. Some of the constables and administrative staff stopped what they were doing. They always enjoyed it when someone else was in the shit with the Colonel.

"Yes, sir! What can I do for you, sir?" Nico asked, once inside his boss's office and the door closed behind him. He had no intention of providing entertainment for the masses.

"You can tell me why we haven't got a certain serial killer in custody yet?"

"I'm working on it, sir."

"Work faster. Look Van Staaden, I know you like to pull the lone wolf crap but if you don't bring me a suspect soon I'll put someone else on the case who is a team player. Do you understand me?"

"Yes sir."

"Good. I want a briefing tomorrow morning, first thing, on what's happening with the case and why we haven't got a suspect in custody yet."

"Yes, sir. Would first thing in the morning be my first thing or yours?"

"What, Captain?"

"Well ... Sir, my first thing is around six-thirty and yours appears to be closer to nine."

"Don't get cute with me, Captain."

"I wouldn't dream of it, sir."

"Be here at nine."

"Yes, sir."

"Now get out of my office."

"Yes, sir."

Nico turned and walked out of the room and bumped straight into Louis.

"Where'd you disappear to?" Louis asked.

"Sorry, but I ..." Nico's sentence was interrupted by Molwedi.

"Who is this and what is he doing here?" he asked, as he poked his head out of his door.

"Sir, this is Louis Gouws. He's a friend of mine and wanted to see where it all happens."

"Captain, this isn't Gold Reef City and we don't do tours. If you wanted to be a tour guide you should have gone into tourism and not the police service. Now kindly get this civilian out of my station."

"Yes, sir," Nico waited for his boss to step back inside his office and slam the door. He turned to Louis. "I think that beer would go down very well right now."

"Shall we go to that pub around the corner from here?"

"*Ja*, what's it called?"

"I haven't got a clue. All I know is that they serve nice cold ones."

"Then lead the way."

*

The pub around the corner turned out to be called Mickey's. Louis and Nico crammed themselves in at the bar, next to a couple of bikers. Probably members of the Max Gang, Nico thought. A rougher crowd hung out here. He recognised a few faces: people who'd found themselves on the wrong side of the law.

"What'll it be?" the barman asked. Nico noticed that he had a tattoo of a spider on his neck.

"Two Black Labels," Louis ordered for them.

He didn't know if it was the atmosphere in the bar, or Louis, or the fact that he'd just let a potential suspect slip through his fingers but Nico was on edge. Something wasn't sitting well with his gut. He watched Louis survey the room. There was something about Louis that he didn't like.

"How did you meet Natalie?" Nico asked, hoping to get to know this man, who'd been a part of Janet's life since childhood. Maybe getting to know him better would silence his suspicion of him. Maybe it was jealousy he felt. That had to be it, he thought, he was jealous of Louis. The realisation was not one of his proudest moments. He hated being jealous.

"We met at Clapham. It was the first day of High school. She was this little waif of a thing. She had orphan practically tattooed on her forehead and some of the other kids picked up on it. Kids being kids, they picked on her, she looked so small and fragile. Janet stepped in, put her arm around her and led her away. Janet was always looking out for her. She was always classy like that." The warmth in Louis's voice when he mentioned Janet made Nico bridle. He wondered if anything had ever happened between the two of them.

"And where were you when this was going on?" Nico asked, instead of the question he was burning to ask.

"I wish I could say that I was as noble as Janet. I was one of the kids who sensed weakness and went for the jugular. Luckily she forgave me for being a dick. Nats had a really rough time at the orphanage. Janet convinced me to help mount a rescue operation one night and after that the three of us were pretty much inseparable."

"And you and Janet never went out?" He regretted asking the moment the question left his mouth and dreaded the answer.

"Nah. She knew how Nats felt about me from the word go and would never do anything to hurt her."

The answer stung. Was Natalie the only reason that they'd never been a couple? Fool! He admonished himself for worrying about something that had never happened. He and Janet were solid. He had no reason to feel jealous but, he still couldn't shake that gut feeling that something was not right. He'd have to keep an eye on Louis Gouws.

9

The rain pelted against the window. It was strange weather for this time of year. Winters in Pretoria were normally brown and dry but then again, nothing about the last five weeks had been normal. Nico watched the lightning split the sky from the safety of the lounge window in his seventh floor flat in Weavind Park. Another Sunday night was upon him. He turned his back on the deluge outside and tried to get the storm raging inside under control.

He watched Janet's rhythmic breathing as she slept curled up on his old couch. His gaze turned to the framed photo hanging on the wall opposite him. It had Police College class of 1989 written in white letters on a blackboard at the feet of the two young men sitting in the front row. Actually they weren't men, they were still boys. Boys sent out to do a man's job. He had been eighteen and had believed he could change things. He had believed he would be able to catch the man who had brutally murdered his mother. Instead he'd ended up in Unit 19, the riot squad, towards the end of the Apartheid era. The things he'd seen and done still haunted him. No teenager should be given an R1 rifle and told to kill people because of the colour of their skin. He was one of the few in his unit to use the R1 rifle which had been copied from the FN FAL, the Belgian Assault Rifle, by the Apartheid regime, after the arms embargo was enforced. The weight of it depended on how far he had to carry it: either fucking heavy or Oh Shit! I'm out of ammo.

The thought of his mother and his time in the townships brought the unpleasant memories from his childhood back like a tidal wave. He was sixteen and in standard eight or what was now referred to as the tenth grade. The new school system still confused him. He had been in detention for smoking behind the school hall and as a result got home later than normal. When he arrived home he opened the garage to put his bicycle inside, next to his mother's car. He switched on the garage light. Her bare feet dangled in front of his face. A dining room chair stood next to her car in the corner of the garage. The man who'd raped and murdered her had hanged her from the rafter closest to the garage door. Her torn dress only just covered her abused body, thanks to a thin strap that clung to her shoulder and refused to drop.

He froze and couldn't comprehend what was happening. He screamed. The next thing he knew there was a policeman standing over him and asking him if he was all right. Of course he wasn't all right. His mother was dead. The police left her body hanging from the rafter while they took photographs of her and poked around inside their home. The policeman who had asked him if he was okay, dragged him to a police car and told him to wait there. He fell asleep in that hot, stinking police car and woke up, an hour later, thinking he'd had the worst nightmare of his life only to find out that it hadn't been a dream at all. He woke up just in time to watch them take her body down.

They drove him to the Silverton Police station where they asked him questions about his mother and her friends. They asked him if she had a boyfriend or if she ever had any men over. He couldn't remember any men. There hadn't been a man in his mother's life since his father died. Her neck had broken when the rapist removed the chair she had been standing on. Having that as the final image of his mother in his mind had scarred him far worse than anything he'd seen and done during his time in Unit 19.

Janet let out a little grunt in her sleep and kindly brought him back to the present. His mother's death was something he tried not to dwell on. He never talked about it and had not told Janet about it. The police had never found her rapist and executioner. He decided, that day in the police car, that he would put murderers and rapists behind bars for as long as possible. But, since then, he'd learnt that things didn't always work out that way. It was a losing battle. The criminals were winning the war on crime.

He found himself in the picture and didn't recognise himself in the boy sitting in the third row. He didn't look like that eighteen-year-old and he didn't remember who that young boy was anymore. So much had happened in the last twenty years. The boy in the picture was innocent. He, on the other hand, had seen too much death and had blood on his hands.

Janet let out another grunt, rolled over on to her back and almost fell off the couch in the process. She sat up, rubbed her eyes, stretched and smothered a yawn. A smile crept across his face as he watched her.

"How long was I out?" she asked through another yawn.

"A while."

"Shit, I'm sorry."

"Don't worry about it. I enjoyed watching you sleep. I especially enjoyed the orchestra."

"Huh? What orchestra?"

"Who knew that such a loud noise could come out of such a small body?"

"You lie! I don't snore." She picked up one of the brown cushions her head had been snuggled into just moments before and flung it at him. It missed its target, bounced off the window and landed at his feet. He picked it up and threw it at her. She managed to catch it millimetres from the tip of her nose.

"Good reflexes. Too bad about that throwing arm," Nico said, with mock surprise in his voice.

"What can I say? When you're good, you're good, and as for the arm … well … who needs that when you look like me?" A smile beamed across her face and crinkled the lines left by the rough fabric of the cushions. She stifled another yawn. The joy Janet gave him was only a temporary escape from his pain and guilt. He turned around and started watching the storm again. He felt helpless. The knowledge that another woman would die tonight made him want to smash the window in front of him. But the next time he wouldn't fail. He made a solemn promise to himself the bastard would pay for each and every one of the lives he had taken.

He felt Janet come up behind him and wrap her arms around his ample stomach.

"Are you okay?" she asked him, propping her chin on his shoulder.

"*Ja!* I'm fine," he said staring out of the window.

"No, you're not." She turned him around so that he faced her. "Talk to me."

"Honestly. I don't want to talk about it. I just want to enjoy being with you," he said and kissed her first on her lips, then the tip of her nose which the cushion had so narrowly missed. He kissed her eyelids and worked his way back to her mouth. He wanted to forget the job and all the shit that went with it. He wanted to be inside her. He needed her to distract him from the ghosts of the dead women he'd failed to protect. But even as his lips were working their way along her face, his mind kept turning to a faceless woman floating in a bath tub.

*

Tonight was the night. He had to do it. He had to end it tonight.

His feet were heavy and felt as though they were dragging on the floor as he walked to her door. Her mongrel dog nuzzled his crotch in greeting. The dog was the only thing that was happy to see him whenever he came here. He took the keys to the front door out of his pocket with shaky hands. Her laughter bounced around inside his head.

"You're pathetic!" Her laughter punctuated every word. "Look at you, shaking in your boots like the chicken shit you are."

He cupped his hands over his ears, trying to shut her out. He had tried to get her out of his head so many times and in so many ways, but it never worked. The only way he could get her voice out of his head was to shut her up permanently.

He remembered finding Natalie lying on the bathroom floor. Her blood spread around her on the white tiles like red silk. He could still see her looking at him with her strange hazel and gold eyes. There had been so much pain in them.

That fucking Bitch had known what it would do to Natalie and she had done it just to hurt him. The front door opened.

"What are you doing standing outside looking like a lost fart?" his mother asked him.

"I just got here, Ma," he said, his voice sounding hoarse, the house keys rattling in his shaking hands. He could smell the same old reek of whisky on her breath. But why wouldn't he? It had been the same ever since he was a small boy.

Every Sunday she would drink herself into a stupor, beat him and lock him in the bathroom. While he lay on the cold floor she thumped on the piano until she was bored. She would finish the bottle of whisky or whatever alcohol she could get her claws on and would open the bathroom door. It was at this point that the real horror would start.

It only became a horror when he was old enough to know that it was wrong. When he had been a boy it had been the only way that his mother had shown him that she loved him. It had been a welcome change to being beaten and he'd always thought that it was her way of saying she was sorry for what she'd done.

"How's that pathetic little whore of yours?" His mother's voice jolted him out of his memory.

"She's not a whore, Ma."

"Yes, she is. You're not married. You are living in sin. No decent woman would live with a man who isn't her husband."

"Ma, stop it. I'm the only man she has ever been with and just because a pastor hasn't married us, doesn't mean she isn't my wife in every other sense of the word. She's the only woman I want."

"But she isn't the only woman you've had now, is she?"

"Stop it, Ma."

"Why? Does the memory turn you on? You pathetic excuse for a man. You probably don't satisfy that whore of yours, either."

Her laughter floated all around him. The room started to turn, slowly. He tried to block out her voice but it just kept coming at him.

"You should have been there when I told that pathetic

little slut of yours that she wasn't the only woman you'd had … that when you were still in high school and she wouldn't put out, you would come home after being with her, all hot under the collar, and I would be here … waiting. And let's not forget about little Janet. You two have been going at it behind her scrawny little back for years."

He lost it. All he could see was Natalie lying in her own blood, accusing him.

His fist flew out and hit her. Her head hit the coffee table with a thunk. He kicked her the way she had kicked him for so many years. She tried to get up, but he struck a blow to the back of her head sending her sprawling to the floor at his feet once again.

Taking the piano wire out of his pocket, he pulled it tight between his hands. A groan escaped from her split and bloodied lips. He looked down at his mother curled up in pain at his feet and kicked her again. His foot connected with her stomach. She gasped for breath. In her struggle to breathe she started throwing up. The bottle of whisky she had finished moments before he arrived rebelled against the beating. With every breath she tried to take, fresh bile and blood appeared in her mouth.

"You're the Bathroom Strangler, aren't you?" Droplets of blood sprayed out of her mouth as she asked the inevitable question. Fear rising in the sound of her voice. The fear she felt was intoxicating for him. It pushed him onwards.

"Please," she begged. "Don't. I'm your mother. I love you." The words came between blood spattered gasps for air.

"No Ma, you don't love me. You never have. The only thing you know how to do is hate. You've taught me to hate you and now you're going to die the way you deserve."

He smiled as he watched her struggle to get on to her hands and knees. Being on her hands and knees made his task easier: it meant he didn't have to move her overweight body into position. She did all the work for him. That's what mothers are for he reflected. He straddled her as though he were riding a horse. The garrotte was already pulled tightly between his fists. He crossed his wrists, looped it over her head and under her chin and pulled her up into a kneeling position between his legs.

She tried to pull the wire away from her throat, but her fingers couldn't get a grip on it. Pleading and incoherent words escaped from her lips while she struggled against him.

"What's the matter, Ma? I thought you liked being on your knees in front of me," he said as he jerked the wire through her throat. Blood gurgled out of the slit in her neck as the wire severed her artery. He was almost disappointed when she stopped struggling and her body went limp. It took about fourteen seconds for her to die.

"You always were a tough old bird," he said between breaths. He slipped the wire out of the gash in her throat. Blood ran down the front of her dress turning the pink floral pattern on her dress red.

*

At home, after his Sunday night visit to his mother, he went straight to the kitchen. He took his uniform out of his backpack and shoved it into the washing machine. He watched the round window in front of the machine fill with water. He heard Natalie's feet padding down the passage towards him and walked out of the kitchen, turned off the light and intercepted her at the door. She was wearing a white nightshirt. Her hair hung loose over her shoulders and was slightly tousled from lying in bed waiting for him.

"Why do you do that?" she asked him.

"Do what?"

"Change out of your uniform after you've been to your mother's. Why do you have clean clothes on before you get home?" she said, counting the questions off on her hand. "Why don't you let me wash your uniform with the rest of your clothes and finally, why do you shove it into the machine the moment you get home?"

"Slow down. Too many questions and it's too late in the evening to be worrying about that kind of shit. I need a shower."

"Why?"

"I need to wash all that filth off me after being at my mother's. Now, go to bed. I'll see you just now."

"But ..." Louis put up his hand to silence her and walked past her into the bathroom. Closing the door behind him, he turned on the shower taps. The hot water pounded against his body. He couldn't believe it. He was finally free of the woman he'd called mother. He could start afresh with Natalie. He could make her happy. He knew he could, especially now that the evil witch was out of the way. Nothing stood in his way. Except one little thing; that bloody woman had seen to that.

The cat was scratching and mewing outside the shower. She was disturbing his moment of reflection. He stepped out of the shower, tripped over the cat and bashed his shin on the toilet bowl.

"Fucking cat!" he growled and kicked it, sending her reeling across the tiles. She smacked head first into the closed bathroom door. He gripped the cat by the scruff of her neck opened the bathroom door, threw her out and slammed the door behind her. He hated cats. Dogs he could handle but cats were disgusting creatures. The memory of drowning the next door neighbour's kitty in the pool put a smile on his face.

The fucking thing had scratched him. After that it had all happened quickly and as though he was watching from a distance. Before he knew what he was doing the cat was under water, struggling for its pathetic life, but he'd had the power over it. He was stronger. After a while he didn't feel its claws scratching at him. He just held it down and kept holding it down. He didn't know when it stopped fighting for its life, but it did. He buried it at the bottom of the garden as a reminder to his own strength.

He was still smiling as he pulled a clean green towel off the rack and dried himself. It was a pleasure rubbing himself, hard, with the towel. It made his skin tingle. Afterwards he felt as though he had scrubbed all the blood and dirt away.

He opened the bathroom door and walked out wearing

the towel wrapped around his waist. Natalie stirred in the bedroom. He leaned against the doorframe and watched her lying in bed reading.

"Why are you looking at me like that?" she asked, looking up from her book. .

"You're full of questions tonight, aren't you?"

"Well, call me curious if you like."

"Okay, curious. So ... would you like to get married?"

"What did you just say?"

"I said ... would you like to marry me?"

"Marry you?"

"Yes."

"Are you kidding? Is this some sick joke?"

"You know what? Fuck you, then. That'll teach me to ask the woman I love to marry me. What was I thinking?" He grabbed a pillow off the bed. His movement towards the bed was fast and made her flinch.

"I'll sleep on the couch tonight. The thought of being in the same bed as you makes me want to throw up," he said and skulked out of the room

"Louis, wait," she said, struggling to get out of the bed.

He slammed the door behind him. Natalie managed to untangle her feet from the duvet and stumbled off the bed towards the door. She opened it and followed him into the lounge where Louis was throwing the pillow on one end of the couch and pounding it with his fist.

"What's really going on?" she asked him, staring at his clenched fists.

"It's something my mother said tonight."

"What did that evil witch say that would prompt a marriage proposal?"

"She called you a whore."

"I see." Tears welled up in her eyes. "So you want to marry a whore, is that it?"

"No! That's not it, you stupid bloody woman." He watched the tears running down her face and enjoyed the same sense of power he'd felt a short while ago, slitting his mother's throat. "I wanted to prove her wrong and make an honest woman out of you."

"I am an honest woman. I don't need some wedding ring on my finger to prove it." She sniffed between her words. The sniffs became sobs. "And who is that bitch to say what makes an honest woman. She sure as hell isn't one."

"Well, she isn't the problem. The fact is that you don't love me enough to marry me."

"I do love you and I've proved that. Remember? I wanted to die when I found out what she did to you. But as long as she's in our lives, it'll be impossible for us to get married. Living together has been hard enough with all her interfering. I don't want our kids to be exposed to that woman."

"She's not a problem anymore."

"The only way she won't be a problem is if she's six feet under and pushing up daisies."

He crooked his left-hand forefinger over his mouth to cover his smile.

"Just trust me when I say she's out of our lives for good," he said as he walked across the room towards her. "Okay?"

"What did you do to get her out of our lives? We've tried before and it's never worked. Why now?"

"Just trust me. She's out of our lives. That's all there is to it. Okay?"

She nodded her head, tears running down her cheeks. He cupped her face in his hands and used his thumbs to wipe away her tears.

"So, can we please just get married now?" he asked.

"There's another problem," she said pushing him away.

"What other problem could there possibly be?"

"How can I ever trust you after ... you and Janet ..." she turned away from him. "Oh god, I can't even say it."

"What did that fucking-interfering-bitch-of-a-friend say happened between us?" Grabbing her by the shoulders he flung her around to face him. This revelation threw him and he knew he had to make sure that Janet couldn't fuck up any of his plans.

"Janet didn't say anything. Your mother took great pleasure in telling me everything."

"She lied, baby. I promise nothing happened between Janet and me." He tipped up her chin using his index finger, forcing her to look at him. "Do you believe me?"

She nodded her head, but didn't meet his eyes.

"So marry me. Don't let my mother screw this up for us with her lies."

"Okay, I'll marry you," she croaked while nodding her head and sobbing.

10

Nico was sitting at his desk in his fishbowl on Tuesday morning when his phone rang. He hated his phone. Whenever it rang it meant there was bad news. The two Lieutenant Colonels, one sitting underneath the window facing the outside world and the other opposite Nico, watched him eyeball his phone. He decided to answer it after eight rings. Irritating the other two officers was an added bonus.

Another body had been found in Weavind Park just a few streets down from the block of flats where he lived. He took down the address from the constable on the other end of the phone. Laurel and Hardy were still watching him when he put down the handset.

"Don't you guys have your own murder cases?" Nico asked as he tore the address off the pad.

"Hey, watch your step Van Staaden. One of these days that attitude of yours is going to get you suspended," Laurel said. His policeman's moustache bristled below a beak of a nose.

"Well, if I do get suspended I won't have to see your ugly face everyday," Nico retorted. Hardy, who sat opposite Nico, gave him a once-over scan with his beady hazel eyes which were hidden behind chubby cheeks, grunted, and then turned his gaze back to the paperwork on his desk.

Nico walked out of the charge office and took the same Nissan Almera he had used for the last crime scene. Luckily he had remembered to empty out the Valpré bottle, otherwise the car would have reeked of urine. He turned on the siren and flashing blue light which looked like an orphan disco light sitting on his dash board. The siren blared all the way through the centre of Pretoria to the eastern suburbs. He loved that siren. Cars always moved out of his way and peak-hour traffic ceased to be a problem whenever he let the siren sing. The victim's house was the second house from the corner of Hartley and De Bruyn Street, on the way to the National Prosecuting Authority offices.

The front garden looked unkempt and was dominated by an old oak tree. Weeds had strangled what was left of the lawn and where there weren't weeds, there was mud and sand. The walls of the house, once white, were now grey and splattered with dry mud. Deep cracks webbed the plaster and the front door hadn't been varnished in years.

"Well, this looks about right for our boy," Nico mumbled to himself, as he got out of the car and walked across the road. A mangy dog, which could only be called a Pavement Special, was barking and jumping against the fence trying to defend its territory against the police. Nico watched the dog's antics with mild amusement. The diversion developed into a question itching in the back of his mind. How did the killer get past the dog?

It took a few minutes for the police to get the dog under control and on its way to the SPCA. He hoped they found it a new home. The usual crowd of inquisitive neighbours started gathering around the property. Nico made his way through the crowd and a sergeant with short, curly red hair opened the gate for him. Pete was talking to a young woman in a pink maid's uniform. Nico made his way towards them. Dr. Papenfuss introduced the woman as Maria. She'd found the body when she went into the bathroom to clean it. She cleaned once a week and the only thing Maria had to say about her employer was that she was a vicious old drunk who lived like a pig and wouldn't let her put anything away. The maid had ranted on for what seemed like an age.

Nico and Pete waited for Thabiso to finish taking pictures of the house, its surrounding area and pictures of the crowd. At the front door, before going in, they put on the usual rubber gloves and protective shoe covers. As they walked in through the front door they saw something that they hadn't seen at any of the other crime scenes.

A Görse & Kalmann piano dominated the dark narrow passage leading into the rest of the house. The piano set off little alarm bells in Nico's head. Past experience had taught

Nico to listen to those bells. He followed his instinct and opened the piano lid exposing the black and white keys. The white keys were starting to turn yellow from age. He ran his fingers along the notes. One of them didn't work. He pressed the black key down a few more times but no sound escaped from the piano. Pete came close to the piano.

"That's E sharp," he said. "Or F natural if you want to get technical."

"Are you sure?" Nico asked, with a raised eyebrow and a racing heart.

"Yes," Pete said. "I've played a bit of piano in my time and that's the right note."

"I wonder," Nico mumbled. He picked up the black-and-white framed picture on top of the piano. The man in the picture looked familiar. He handed Pete the picture and opened the top panel to expose the inner mechanics. There were what looked like baby's bootie-shaped pieces of wood attached to thin wires. The wires glinted in the darkness. He picked up his torch, switched it on and shone the light into the dark cavern, illuminating the wires. Nico pushed down a few other keys and watched the bootie-shapes tapping against the wires, causing notes to emanate from the piano. He tapped the E sharp key. Nothing happened: the wood didn't move. He shone the beam of the torch in the place where he guessed the E sharp wire would be. He saw the reason why no sound escaped. The wire was missing.

"So, who was this woman?" Nico asked Pete, while repeatedly pushing the E sharp key down.

"Marietta Gouws, fifty-five-years-old, divorced with one child ... a son called Louis." He read from his well-used notebook.

"Did you say Louis Gouws?"

"*Ja*, why?"

"Does he work for Rent-a-cop?"

"Yes. How'd you know that?"

"I know him. He's an old friend of Janet's."

"Well, that's interesting. He was seen leaving here on Sunday night."

"So Louis was seen leaving here last night?" Nico kept tapping the dead note.

"Yes, that's what they tell me."

"That's quite interesting, wouldn't you say? Mother and son ... son has a career in security. The rent-a-cop uniform looks remarkably like a standard police uniform and I wonder how much he knows about forensics and police procedure."

"That's a fascinating train of thought – are you sure it's one you want to pursue?"

"Why wouldn't I?"

"Well, for one thing, this guy's your buddy."

"He's not my buddy. I haven't known him for very long: I've only had a couple beers with the guy."

"Okay, but your girlfriend has known him for a while. How will she feel if you go after her friend in a murder investigation?"

"Firstly, I go where the evidence leads me, she knows that and secondly, Janet doesn't like the guy. She thinks he's an arsehole."

"And what if you're wrong?"

"I'm not wrong. There's something about this guy. You don't normally tell me to ignore the bells going off in my head or second guess my gut instinct."

"No, that's not what I'm saying. *If* we've found our guy we need more than your gut instinct and circumstantial evidence to put him away. "

"Then what are you saying?"

"All I'm saying is that we should be careful. Keep an eye on him, but don't let him know that we're watching him. Okay?"

"Okay."

"Good and now that that's settled, I believe we still have the rest of the crime scene to walk. Captain, if you're finished playing with the piano?"

"Hmm ..." Nico grunted, pulled himself away from the piano and tried to push all thoughts out of his mind so that he could concentrate on the job at hand. He took another glance at the picture on the piano. The man was obviously Louis's father. The resemblance between father and son was uncanny. He focused on what he had to do. He would deal with telling Louis about his mother's death first and the questions tugging at his gut, later.

In the lounge there was a puddle of blood on the carpet and on the coffee table. Thabiso took photos from all corners of the room and from 90-degree angles. He also took photos from directly above each piece of potential evidence as well as all the blood splatter. Nico took a sweeping glance at the rooms in the house. The thing that struck Nico the most was that there were no pictures of her son. He filed this fact along with everything else that was bugging him about this case.

As with all the other scenes, the blood trail led from the room where she was killed to the bathroom. Marietta Gouws was lying in the bathtub, much the same as the other victims before her. Deep cuts on her fingertips, from when she had tried to grip the wire to pull it away from her throat, had practically sliced off her finger prints. The flashes from Thabiso's camera were fraying his nerve endings. Every time he tried to seize hold of an elusive thought, the camera flash would go off and he would loose his train of thought.

He'd seen enough. He wanted to be able to go to the other victims' family members, tell them that the man who had killed their mothers was behind bars and would never be able to hurt anybody else ever again. He also wanted to see how Louis would react to the news of his mother's death. Perhaps he was the murdering bastard he would end up putting away.

But first he had something else to take care of and hopefully, by the end of the night, he would have the answers he needed.

*

Nico sat in his car, parked a few houses down from Marietta Gouws' home. He'd parked under the shade of a big stinkwood tree after everybody left the scene, which took several hours to process. It was now late in the day and he hoped that his suspect was desperate enough to show up to collect his trophy.

Something else that bugged Nico about this was, why did the killer come back for the trophy. Why didn't he take it when he killed her? Did he get an extra thrill going there after the police had been on the scene? There were too many things that didn't make sense. The piano in Marietta Gouws's house with a missing wire was just another part of the puzzle he didn't like and he wasn't sure how he felt about the direction in which it was pointing. If Louis was the killer it could put strain on his relationship with Janet. What if Janet didn't believe him? What if she decided to believe in Louis's innocence, even in the face of irrefutable evidence? But he was jumping the gun. He didn't even know for sure that Louis was guilty. He would have to cross that bridge with Janet when they got there.

Nico had been sitting in the car for almost two hours. His arse was starting to go numb, he needed to relieve himself and, worst of all, he was bored. He was also starting to think he'd made a right royal fuck-up and the killer wasn't going to show. Another Radio Jacaranda DJ was being obnoxious and irritating him. The radio was, unfortunately, his only company. This time around he had come prepared for a long wait. He had an empty one-and-a-half litre Valpré bottle, snacks and coffee in a thermos flask. The coffee had been an inspired idea. He took a swig: it was black and sweet. When he had been a toddler and at nursery school, the woman who ran the nursery school had left their chocolate milk out in the sun. It had gone sour and she forced him to drink it anyway. The memory of having to drink it resurrected a horrible taste in his mouth. His mother had tried to get him to drink milk after that but he'd clamped his mouth shut and refused to drink it. She eventually gave up. He had always been stubborn. It was this quality that made him a good detective.

The sun started to set and dropped below his line of sight. Street lights flashed on above his car. A green Toyota Tazz drove past and Nico ducked down onto the passenger seat. The Toyota kept driving. Nico sat up straight again in his seat once the Toyota's headlights had disappeared around the corner. The temperature dropped and the wind picked up.

He watched another car come round the corner into Hartley Street and turn left into De Bruyn Street on its way home. He wished that he was on his way home but, still had a long night ahead of him. His cell phone rang and vibrated against his thigh. He lifted up his left hip so he could get his hand into the trouser pocket. He recognized Janet's number and realised he was going to be in trouble.

"Where are you?" she said the moment he answered. He could hear that she was trying to sound calm but worry, tinged with anger, crept into her voice.

"I'm sitting in my car outside a victim's house."

"What do you mean sitting in your car? You were supposed to be here over an hour ago!" She used her angry voice, with only a slight hint of worry.

"I'm sorry, sweetie, I've got to work tonight."

"Why didn't you call me? Or is that asking too much?"

Now he knew he was in big trouble. A storm front was definitely on the rise. Headlights headed in his direction. He ducked. Janet's voice shouted at him from the cell phone. The headlights didn't drive past or turn into any other street. He peered over his steering wheel to see where the car had stopped. His heart pounded in his chest and the adrenalin pumped through his veins. The car stopped right outside Marietta Gouws's home.

He couldn't believe his luck. The killer was either incredibly stupid or desperate, or both. The headlights were switched off and the same blond head from the Entabeni flats emerged from the car. It was the same white Golf.

"Nico, are you still there?" Janet's voice interrupted his excitement.

"Have to go," he said and hit the disconnect button before she could say anything. An action which would put him in hot water when he went home.

Nico waited for his suspect to open the gate and walk to the front door. This time there wasn't anywhere for him to run. Nico knew he finally had the bastard. The feeling of triumph started to rise in the pit of his stomach. But the nagging feeling this was all too easy tugged at the back of his mind.

He watched his suspect open the front door and made a mental note to find out how the suspect had obtained a set of keys for the house. Nico waited for him to go inside and then got out of his car. Closing the car door softly behind him, he removed his 9mm service pistol from his hip holster. Crouching, he ran across the road, his gun at the ready and jumped over the wire fence. Good thing it was only waist high, he thought, as he landed in the garden. All the other fences and walls in the neighbourhood were well over six feet high and sported razor wire on top. He sprinted across the garden and crouched against the wall at the front door. He decided this was as good a place as any to wait for his suspect to come out. It was dark and the walls of the house cast a dark shadow over him.

He was down on his haunches with his pistol gripped firmly in front of him when he heard his suspect opening the front door. With heart pounding and hands sweating, he waited for his suspect to walk past him before he made his move.

"Police!" Nico shouted, as he came out of the crouch. "Stop right there!"

His suspect stopped mid-stride. Nico felt as though time was standing still. The suspect hesitated and then broke into a sprint. Nico took aim and fired. The man stopped running, the warning shot had landed at his feet.

"There's no where to run. You might as well cooperate or the next bullet won't end up in the ground." The suspect nodded his head and his body slumped in surrender.

"Put your hands up, slowly, above your head." He did as he was told, a silver candlestick in need of a polish in his hand. Nico walked slowly towards him, ready to fire his pistol if the man moved a muscle. Nico stood behind him and removed his pistol from his hip holster and then patted him down for more weapons and found a second, non-issue, revolver strapped to his ankle and removed it. Putting the nuzzle of his pistol at the base of the suspect's skull, Nico pulled out his handcuffs and placed them in the man's hands

"Put them on," Nico instructed.

"Can I move my hands?" the suspect asked, his voice sounded young, too young to belong to a serial killer, but age wasn't a determining factor for a monster.

"Don't try to be funny. Just put them on," Nico said as he applied more pressure with the barrel of his pistol. He heard the handcuffs click into place.

"Now turn around. No sudden movements."

As his suspect turned around slowly, Nico recognised the man he had been hunting. He had been under his nose the whole time. It was the bored young constable who had pissed him off at all the murder scenes.

"According to section thirty five of the Constitution you're under arrest, Constable, for the murders of Michelle Venter, Amanda Du Plessis, Theresa van Wyk, Erica Steenkamp ..."

"Hey! Wait a moment, I didn't do that! I didn't kill anybody, Captain." The young constable looked frightened and confused.

"I suggest you shut your trap and talk to a lawyer. Now where was I? Oh yes ... furthermore, I arrest you for the murders of Tanya McKenzie and Marietta Gouws. You have the right to remain silent." He made sure that the handcuffs were tight enough. "You have the right to legal representation. If you cannot afford legal representation, someone will be appointed to you by the State. Anything you say can and will be used against you in a court of law. Do you understand these rights as I have read them to you?" Nico said, while he marched the constable over to his car.

"I swear, Captain, I didn't kill those women. I just had a few debts to pay so I pinched some things so that I could flog them. I'm not a killer. I'm just a thief."

"Save it for your lawyer, fuck nut. I really don't want to hear it," Nico said and pushed him into the back seat of the car. Nico slid into the front seat and radioed in to the station that he was bringing in a suspect for the Bathroom Strangler case. He was in for a long night of paperwork and Janet was going to put him on dry rations for at least a month for standing her up. Not to mention what she would do to him for hanging up on her.

*

It was almost midnight when Nico buzzed Louis's and Natalie's flat in Sunnyside. He could have waited till morning and given Louis a decent night's sleep: but there was still something about Louis and the whole case which bothered him. He hoped surprising him in the middle of the night would catch him off his guard.

The paperwork and interviewing the constable had taken a few hours and taken their toll on Nico. He was exhausted. He had delegated someone to check on the cop's alibis for all the murders. It was something he would have preferred doing himself but he needed to confront his suspicions about Louis, so he could move on with the case. He only hoped everybody at the station had respected his request and not yet informed Louis of his mother's death. He wanted to see the expression on Louis's face as he gave him the news.

Louis's sleep-filled voice answered the buzzer.

"This had better be good!"

"It's Nico."

"What are you doing here? Do you have any idea what time it is?"

"I'm sorry but it's important."

There was a buzzing sound and the gate clicked open. This was usually the part of his job he hated the most. The dead bodies and the criminals he could handle. Telling a person that someone they loved was never coming home was a whole other story. But this time, it felt like a game of cat and mouse.

Louis was standing in the corridor outside his flat when Nico stepped out of the lift. The light above the door was bright and Nico could see that Louis was still trying to adjust his drowsy eyes to the light. Louis only had his pyjama pants on and goose flesh had started to crawl across his chest.

"Let's go inside," Nico said to a confused-looking Louis.

Louis turned without saying a word and led the way back into the flat. Natalie was in the kitchen wearing a white terry-towelling gown greying with age and big, fluffy animal slippers on her feet. She yawned while filling the kettle with water.

"I thought a cup of coffee might be a good idea," she said when they walked into the kitchen.

"So, what's so important that you had to get us out of bed at this time of night?" Louis asked him, stifling a yawn.

"I'm sorry to do this to you and I don't know how to tell you this to be quite honest," Nico said, combing his fingers through his thinning hair.

"Well, you've woken us up now, so you might as well just spill it," Louis said.

Somewhere car brakes screeched to a halt and hooters blared. There was a period of silence that seemed to last forever as Nico tried to think about the best way to do this. The speech he had been preparing on his way up evaporated the instant he walked through the door. The kettle boiled and Natalie poured the boiling water into three mugs and put the mugs on the kitchen table in front of them. She sat down next to Louis and sipped her coffee in silence. Her actions were slow, and deliberate, almost calculated.

"I've got some bad news for you and umm ... *ag*, shit ... the thing is ... well, it's your mother."

Natalie's eyebrow twitched.

"What about her?" Louis said and then took a sip of his coffee. Nico wasn't sure how to read the expression on his face. Something flashed across his eyes but Nico wondered if he was just looking for something that wasn't there.

"I'm sorry to have to be the one to tell you this ... but she was found dead yesterday."

There was a long silence. He could hear cars driving past in the busy streets outside. The one thing about Sunnyside was that it never slept. There was always something going down in this part of the city. Someone was probably being murdered or robbed just a few blocks away. The murder and robbery unit were trying their hardest to crack down on the area and were, surprisingly, making headway. They had made some large drug busts in the last few months that had made front-page news. It had been very good PR for the service.

The look on Natalie's face surprised Nico. She just stared at Louis. There were no tears. She didn't ask how it happened. There was no denial. Neither one of them, for that matter, said that it was impossible. Neither one displayed the first stages of grief. She just sat there and stared at Louis, dumbfounded, with a strange glint in her eyes. It was almost as if she'd expected it. He would have to ask Janet about Natalie's history with Louis's mother. He doubted that Louis would ever tell him what Natalie's story was and he had a feeling that it was a very interesting one. After what seemed an inordinately long silence, Louis collected himself and cleared his throat. Nico pulled his attention away from Natalie and focused on Louis.

"So ... um ... what exactly happened?" Louis's voice croaked.

"She was killed on Sunday night by the Bathroom Strangler. We do have a suspect in custody. I know that's not much consolation but at least you have the satisfaction of knowing that the bastard is behind bars."

"You're right; it isn't any consolation. I can't believe it. I saw her on Sunday night."

"Yes, I know. One of her neighbours saw you go in."

Louis stood up, pushing his chair back as he stood and started pacing the length of the small kitchen.

"I'm ... sorry ... it's just that ... my mother and I had an argument that night. I just stormed out of there ... and now ... If only I had stayed a little longer ... she might still be alive."

"An argument? What was it about?" Nico asked, looking from Louis to Natalie.

"It was about Natalie." Louis stopped pacing, looked down at Nico and crossed his arms. "We argued about her every time I went there. Why are you asking me about this?"

"I'm just trying to get a feel for everything that happened

to your mother on Sunday. How often did you see her?" Nico took out his note pad and started taking notes.

"I visited her every Sunday."

"Every Sunday?"

"Yes, every Sunday. Why do I feel like I'm being interrogated?"

Natalie was still sitting in her chair, dry-eyed and drinking her coffee in silence. Nico's warning bells were clanging and drowned out any other thoughts. Something was very wrong with this picture. He tried to tell himself that maybe she just reacted to shock differently from most people. Maybe he had been a cop for too long and his overly-suspicious mind was playing tricks on him. Maybe Louis was sincere in his grief and he just wasn't seeing it. But those bells kept clanging. The fact that he visited his mother every Sunday just made those bells clang even louder.

His mother was the catalyst. She was the trigger.

"I'm sorry. This isn't an interrogation. I'm just getting the facts. Now back to the argument you had. Why was it about Natalie?"

"They always have arguments about me. His mother hated me." Natalie finally found her voice.

"I told my mother that I was going to ask Natalie to marry me, which I did when I got home," Louis said, taking a few steps forward and standing behind Natalie's chair. He put his hands on her shoulders and started rubbing them.

"Congratulations! I wish it was under better circumstances."

"So do we," Louis said, looking down at Natalie's head.

"There are still a lot of questions that I have to ask but that can wait till tomorrow," Nico said, getting up and walking from the kitchen into the dark entrance hall of their flat. "I'll give you a call later in the day to work out all the details."

"Okay. I'll chat to you then"

"Once again, I'm sorry for your loss," Nico said, stepping into the hallway outside their door.

Nico turned and walked away. He heard the door close behind him and wondered what was being said. He would find out tomorrow if the right man was spending the night in jail. But he had a sneaking suspicion that he'd arrested the wrong man for murder.

*

Once Nico had left and the door was closed behind him, Natalie turned on Louis.

"So is there something you should tell me?" she asked him, her arms wrapped around her chest.

"What the fuck are you on about now, you crazy woman?"

"Oh, I don't know … how about … how you knew that she wouldn't be a problem for us ever again? Huh … How did you know that?"

"Natalie what are you trying to imply?" he asked as he took a few steps closer to her. He was close enough for her to smell his breath. There was still a hint of minty toothpaste on it.

"I'm not implying anything. I'm asking you straight out did you or did you not have something to do with this?"

His laughter was the last thing she had expected. It was deep and guttural. It stopped just as suddenly as it had started.

"So you think I'm the Bathroom Strangler, do you?" He arched his dark thin eyebrows.

"I didn't say that." Her voice had lost its conviction and wasn't much more then a whisper. "It's just that I wouldn't blame you if you *had* killed that horrible cow and made it look like the Bathroom Strangler did it."

"Well, I wish I had but you heard the man. They already have someone in custody." He wrapped his right arm around her waist and pulled her closer to him. "Ding dong the witch is dead." He kissed her hard, forcing her lips apart with his tongue.

11

Nico walked into his fishbowl a few hours later and threw his car keys and cell phone onto his desk. He pulled his jacket off, which felt a little tight around his shoulders and draped it over the back of his office chair. Either all his clothes had shrunk or he needed to go on that diet Janet kept suggesting. Sitting down, he rested his elbows on his government issue desk and rubbed his stubbly chin. A shit day lay ahead of him. There wasn't any proper evidence against the young constable sitting in the holding cells below; most of the evidence he had was circumstantial. Even though he was guilty of theft and perverting the course of justice, he wasn't the killer.

He wasn't looking forward to dealing with Louis. He needed to get all his thoughts down on paper; it was the only way he could sift through everything that was swirling around in his head. He took out a pen and was searching his drawers for paper when his boss, Colonel Molwedi, phoned him.

"Get your white arse into my office now, Van Staaden." The phone was slammed down. His day was off to a very bad start.

It took him a few minutes to get to Molwedi's office. He knocked three times and was answered by "Get in here!"

"So let me guess … I'm in the shit?" Nico said as he walked into the office and closed the door behind him.

"Whatever gave you that impression?" Molwedi said, his hands clutched in front of him on his cluttered desk. Moses Molwedi's desk was typical government issue, only bigger than Nico's. Desk size was the best way to tell the difference in rank in any government department.

"Oh! I don't know … maybe the 'Get your white arse up here' thing. So … what terrible crime against humanity have I committed this time?"

"They are too numerous for me to mention all of them in one sitting."

"Look Boss, can we get this pithy shit out of the way so

you can crap me out for whatever it is and then I can get back to work. How does that sound?"

"I'm going to ignore the fact that you don't enjoy our banter. Now, about this fucked-up arrest you made last night. What were you thinking?"

"Well Boss, I was …"

"Oh, shut up. That was a rhetorical question. I know what you were thinking. Nothing! Absolutely nothing, you weren't thinking at all." Molwedi got up from his chair and started pacing behind his desk.

"Now, what I want to know, Captain, is, haven't you learnt anything about the law of evidence during all your years on the force?"

"Well, considering that I caught the guy with the victim's property in his hands and, sir, I think you mean 'service' don't you? Remember the whole image change?"

"If I were you, I'd watch the attitude. You are this close to a suspension," Molwedi said, holding up his thumb and index finger in a pincer position and less then an inch apart.

"You've threatened that a few times and I've never been suspended, so it would be an interesting experience."

"Then consider yourself suspended."

"Thanks so much for the experience. Now do you want to tell me why you're suspending me, other then my attitude?"

"There's the fact that I just don't like you. You've already got two warnings for insubordination on your permanent file and that fuck-up you called an arrest which you made last night."

"Oh, *ja*, I forgot about those two *minor* incidents. But you've got to admit that Laurel and Hardy, I mean Maritz and Lubbe deserved everything they got and they were just small practical jokes. Who knew that they didn't have a sense of humour?" He noticed that Molwedi shared the same deficiency with Laurel and Hardy, so quickly changed the subject. "But what about last night? Why was it such a colossal fuck-up?"

"All his alibis check out. He's not the Bathroom Strangler. The only thing we can charge him with is theft and obstruction of justice. And thanks to you we have yet another corrupt policeman on our hands. We have enough image problems with corruption as it is. The press are going to have a field day with this. It's a PR nightmare."

"You're kidding me. You're worried about a PR issue. We've taken another corrupt cop off the streets. That's a win for us and no reason to suspend me, you should be giving me a medal."

"You're really starting to get on my tits. Isn't that a good enough reason?"

"No."

"Pity. Okay, the lone wolf act that you keep pulling, your attitude towards your superiors and the fact that you were already on very thin ice. Also, I don't like the way you're handling this case. Your judgement is clouded. This is a high profile case and, considering your past experience with certain members of the press, we need someone who will represent the police effectively in the media. How's *them* for reasons?"

"That's only enough to pull me off the case."

"Which was what I was going to do, then you asked for the suspension. Remember?"

"I forgot about that."

"So, please hand me your police ID and your side arm."

Nico removed his pistol from his hip holster and placed it on Molwedi's desk. He then took his police ID out of his wallet and placed it next to his pistol.

"Here's the official suspension form you need to sign." Molwedi took a form out of his top drawer and pushed it across his desk towards Nico.

"How long is the suspension?" Nico asked, while signing the document.

"A month. Now get out of my sight."

"Yes, sir." Nico turned and walked towards the door, his ego crushed, as well as any will to fight with Molwedi.

"Oh, and Captain – come back with a better attitude. Use the time to learn to be a team player."

"I'll try, sir," Nico said, while opening the door. He stepped out of the office and closed the door behind him.

Once outside Molwedi's office and his earshot he smacked himself on his forehead and shook his head.

"Stupid, stupid, stupid," he said under his breath and leaned against the wall. He needed to think, needed to figure out his next move, especially if he was right about Louis. He could only hope that by killing his mother he had also killed his motivation.

"Yeah, right, someone's definitely living in a dream world," he mumbled to himself. Looking up, he discovered that all eyes from the open-plan office were on him. He straightened his tie and tried to ignore the pounding headache developing at his temples and his ulcer making its presence felt. He wanted to throw up.

Fishing a Tums out of his pocket, he popped it into his mouth and walked along the passage and down the stairs, back to his fishbowl.

Laurel and Hardy ignored his entrance. Nico opened the stationery cupboard the three of them shared and emptied a box of its contents onto the floor. He put the empty box onto his desk, pulled the top drawer out of his desk and tipped the contents into the box. He started to do the same to the second drawer when Louis knocked on the open door.

"Am I interrupting something?" Louis asked, looking at the box.

"No, not really, I'm just emptying out my desk."

"Why?"

"Because I've been suspended?"

"What?"

"I. Have. Just. Been. Suspended," Nico said slowly, enunciating each word for effect.

"I heard you. Shit! Man, I'm sorry but if you're suspended who's handling my mother's murder and you said you had a whole lot of questions you wanted to ask me?"

"I'm sure one of these two jokers will be able to take your statement. If they can pull their fingers out of their arses, that is." Nico said, looking at Laurel and Hardy. "And I'm sure one of them will be taking over as lead detective."

"Why are they suspending you?"

"My attitude sucks," Nico said, emptying the contents of his bottom drawer into the box.

"Oh, okay and umm ... how long are you going to be suspended?"

"A month and then, if my attitude hasn't changed, they'll probably decide to take further disciplinary action."

"I'm sorry, I don't understand."

"It's quite simple: my boss hates my big fat white arse," Nico said as he put the lid back on the box which now contained all his personal belongings. "A lot of guys have been drummed out of the service for less, so I'm pretty lucky I still have a job. It's out with the old and in with the new. The only reason those two boneheads still have a job is because their noses are so far up Molwedi's arse that when he shits, they burp fart."

"So you can just walk away from this without a second glance?"

"No, but I don't have much choice on this one. I'm sorry, Louis, but there's nothing I can do."

Louis sat down on a chair opposite Nico's desk.

"I don't believe this. I was counting on you."

"Would one of you please help this man?" Nico said to Laurel and Hardy, as he picked up his box and walked towards the door. He stopped at the open doorway and turned around. He gave the office one last glance, making sure he hadn't forgotten anything that he couldn't live without. His glance rested on Louis and his stomach wanted to revolt. He hated unfinished business. "Look, if you need anything or if there's anything I can do to help, please give me a call," Nico said and walked out, right into Pete.

"Where're you going with that box?"

"What? Haven't you heard?"

"Heard what?"

"That's right, it's a little too soon for the rumours to have reached all the way to you. I've been suspended."

"I wish I could say it was a surprise. What are you going to do?"

"I haven't got a clue but I need a favour?"

"As long as you don't need cash, then I'm your guy."

"I need you to keep an eye on Louis Gouws for me."

"Of course."

"Thanks and while you're at it, make sure Laurel and Hardy don't just sit on their arses with this one."

"I'll try and I'll keep you posted on how things develop. But if we're right about your friend, I don't think there'll be another murder for a while. He's killed his stressor and for now he'll think he can live a normal life. But the smallest thing will set him off. If he kills again, it'll be in frustration and it'll be worse than the others."

*

The sun was low in the sky when Nico pulled up outside Janet's block of flats. He had driven around most of the day, not quite knowing what to do with himself. Being a policeman had defined who he was for most of his adult life and now that he wasn't one, even if it was only for a month, left him feeling out of sorts.

Janet's green Opel Corsa was parked in its usual spot outside the main entrance. He sat in his own car, a battered old Datsun, staring into space. He had inherited the car from his grandmother shortly after graduating from the Police College. She had been his only relative to live long enough to see him graduate. She died a week later and the car had been the only thing she left him.

There was an annoying tap-tap sound. He ignored it, lost in his own thoughts. The tapping became a loud banging at his window. He looked up to see a rather unhappy Janet scowling back at him. He unlocked his door and got out. Janet's arms were crossed and he could tell by the way she was standing, it was her 'I'm waiting' stance, that his explanation had better be good. It was the first time she'd been this angry with him and, as far as he was concerned, she had never been more desirable. Too bad he wasn't up to it.

"How did you know I was here?"

"I've just got here myself and it's difficult to miss your heap of junk from the entrance."

"I suppose it is your usual time to get home."

"Yes, it's my usual time but it isn't yours. So, what are you doing here?"

"Can we go upstairs? I don't want to talk about it out here."

"Nico, what's going on?" Her voice softened and so did her body language.

"Have you spoken to Natalie today?"

"No, I've been on a course all day. So she wouldn't have been able to get hold of me even if she'd wanted to."

"On a course?"

"Yes, a management course, nothing too fancy. Don't change the subject, why are you asking me if I've spoken to Natalie? What's going on?"

"Let's go inside and I'll explain everything, okay?" he asked, guiding her towards the entrance to her block.

"Okay."

They walked to the block and up the stairs to the first floor in silence. Janet fished around in her oversized handbag for her keys. Nico always wondered what she kept in there and why she needed such a big bag. She opened the door and stepped inside. Nico followed and closed the door behind them. She dropped her bottomless pit of a bag on the dining room table and walked into her kitchen. Nico carried on down the passage into the lounge. He sat down on the red couch carefully. He had learnt that it could suck him under if he wasn't careful. The cushions billowed out around him. Janet came out of the kitchen carrying two glasses of white wine.

"What's that for?" Nico asked her as she walked towards him.

"You look like you could use a drink and this is the strongest I have." She handed him a glass that was too full and on the verge of spilling over.

He took a sip to prevent spillage and then stared at the glass, not knowing where to start.

"So ... do you want to tell me what's going on or do I have to guess?" Janet asked, breaking the silence.

"I don't know where to start."

"How about you start with why you stood me up last night?"

"Oh, *ja*, I did, hey."

"What do you mean 'Oh *ja*, I did, hey.'?" she said mimicking him, with an edge to her voice.

"Sorry, honey. I really am and I do have a decent excuse."

"You bloody well better have."

"Louis's mother was killed on Sunday by the Bathroom Strangler."

"*What?*"

"I was staking out her house last night waiting for the killer to show up. As it turns out, the guy I thought was the killer is a nineteen-year-old snot-nosed constable, who goes back to the victim's homes after we've done everything we have to do and robs the place." He took a breath and a sip of the wine. "Anyway, I arrested the stupid shit and have been suspended for my troubles." He gulped down half the glass in one swig.

"They suspended you just for arresting the guy?"

"Well ... not just for that. My attitude sucks, I'm told; I didn't follow proper procedure; the guy has valid alibis for all the murders; my boss thinks I'm not a team player and I pull too many lone-wolf stunts. I already have two warnings on my file. Plus Molwedi has been gunning for me since he took over that position. I've got the wrong skin colour. Blah blah blah." He gulped the rest of the wine down.

"I see." Janet took a sip of her wine. "how long is the suspension?"

"A month and then Molwedi will decide if my attitude has improved or not."

"So what are you going to do for a month?"

"Nothing. I'm just going to sit on my arse and drive you crazy."

"That's all fine and well, but you can't sit still for two minutes – how the hell are you going to make it through a whole month?"

"As I said, I'm going to drive you nuts." He eyed the empty glass, hoping to find a drop of wine he might have missed. "Oh, I almost forgot. When I was at Louis's place last night telling him about his mother, he told me that he and Natalie are engaged. He proposed on Sunday night."

"Really? Wow. It's strange that she didn't tell me."

"Maybe she couldn't get hold of you – you were on a course – or she just had other things on her mind. You never know with fruitcakes like that."

"She's not a fruitcake."

"Yes, she is. There's definitely something not right with that one."

"Hey, careful there, you're talking about my best friend."

"Sorry Sweetie, but that's another thing I don't understand …"

"What don't you understand?"

"Your friendship with Natalie …"

"What about it?"

"… doesn't make sense. You're both so different."

"So we're different. What's your point?"

"I don't understand how you two could be such good friends when you're such total opposites."

"We're not total opposites."

"Yes, you are. She's a nut and you're not."

"Look, Nats and I have been friends since high school. When we met, some kids were bullying her because she was living in an orphanage. She had nothing, no home, no family and no friends. I felt sorry for her so I stood up for her and we've been friends ever since."

"Now *that* I understand." Nico said, tapping his index finger against the empty glass.

"What do you understand?" she said, getting up from the couch, taking his glass and walking to the kitchen.

"You feeling sorry for her." He raised his voice so that she could hear him in the kitchen. "And you still do."

"She has a lot of issues," Janet called from the kitchen. "So what? Everybody has issues."

"The fact that you feel sorry for her is the foundation of your friendship."

"No, it's not."

"Yes, it is."

"Since you want to discuss strange friendships, how about yours and Louis's? That's a match made in La La Land as far as I'm concerned."

"He's an okay guy," he said taking a sip of his wine and hoping she would drop the Louis issue. He wasn't sure how he'd tell her he thought one of her oldest friends was a serial killer.

"Wait a minute, why have you got that look on your face?'

"What look?"

"That look you get when you want to dodge a topic."

"I have no such look."

"Yes, you do and you have that look right now."

"I do not."

Janet looked at him with arched eyebrows and a grin played on her lips.

"Oh, all right, so I don't want to talk about Louis right now or anything to do with his mother's murder. It has nothing to do with me anymore," Nico said, taking another sip and eyeing her over the rim of the glass.

"Now why don't I believe you?" she said, as she plopped down onto the couch.

"Because you know me too well?"

"Mmmm … Good answer. Now stop dodging and spill it."

"Seriously, I'm not dodging anything but I would like to know more about Natalie and Louis's relationship," he said drinking more of the wine, which was starting to taste like vinegar.

"Why?" Janet asked, crossing and uncrossing her legs.

"I'm just curious, that's all."

"What are you curious about?"

"Well … How did they get together?"

"We all went to the same school together; Natalie had a crush on him from eighth grade. I still don't understand why she's fascinated by him. He was a loner: he had no friends and the only thing he did was play rugby and that was because it was mandatory to do a sport. He just didn't fit in."

"I can see how they would make a perfect match then." He pretended not to see Janet's look of disapproval.

"The three of us somehow ended up as friends. I don't even remember how it happened. But Louis only started thinking of her as more than just a friend in Matric. He noticed how beautiful she is at the Valentine's Day ball. She looked incredible that night; she must have scrimped and saved for ages. I still don't know how she managed to get the money together for that dress. The people at the orphanage were horrible to her and wouldn't do jack-shit to help her. To make a long story short, they've been together ever since."

"Cute story. What was her relationship like with Louis's mother?" He couldn't help but wonder how much of the tale she was leaving out. Was there something she wasn't telling him?

"Is this an interrogation?"

"No, it's not, but I would like to know why you're trying to avoid the subject?" he asked, arching one eyebrow.

"Is that your interrogation face?" she asked him, grinning.

"It is, if it works for you. Now stop avoiding the question. I'm serious, what was Natalie's relationship like with Louis's mother?"

"Okay, fine. It was strained."

"How strained?"

"Louis's mother was a mean, cold-hearted bitch."

"How strained?"

"Why are you being such a cop about this?"

"Why are you avoiding the question?"

"I'm not avoiding it."

"Then answer the question."

"Okay. They hated each other. You happy now?"

"No. Why do you say they hated each other?"

"I don't know all the details, but I do know that Louis's mother is the reason Natalie slit her wrists."

"Wait a minute, the infamous suicide attempt was because of Louis's mother?"

"Apparently, but Natalie won't tell me what happened. It was all really weird. After that she changed."

"An attempted suicide will change you, believe it or not."

"I know that but she changed towards me. I'm probably being paranoid but she just acts differently around me now. It's almost as if she doesn't trust me anymore. She's shut me out." Her lips quivered as she tried to fight back tears.

Nico rubbed his fingertips over the bottom of his chin and scraped them against his two-day stubble. He filed the information away with all the other parts of the puzzle that didn't fit together; he needed to put them all together. Not that it would do him any good at this point, since he was off the case, but he had to finish what he'd started.

*

She couldn't concentrate on any of the contracts her boss had placed in front of her during the day. Luckily he bought the act Natalie laid on thick about her shock and grief over the death of her mother in-law-to-be and let her go home early. She now sat on their second-hand couch, thinking.

The thoughts started out as a jumble but now everything started to make sense. She'd wondered why he worked every Sunday night shift and went to see his mother during his shift. The way he behaved when he got back from those Sunday visits had puzzled her. Before, he would never have touched her after being to see his mother, but the last few weeks they'd had sex every Sunday night. It was as clear as daylight to her now. The gift of twenty-twenty hindsight was an amazing thing. The only thing she didn't know was what to do with this revelation.

She didn't know how she felt. She'd hated that evil witch, but the other women were innocent. Weren't they? Louis must have had a reason for killing them. Maybe they deserved it. She had to admit she didn't care about the other women: they meant nothing to her. They were faceless and generally nameless women, whom the media had branded as a bunch of alcoholics.

She got off the couch, walked to the kitchen and opened the fridge. She glanced inside and slammed it shut without taking anything out. The kitchen clock ticked and the sound grated on her nerves. The traffic outside competed with the ticking clock for most annoying sound. She walked back into the lounge and stared at nothing in particular. Trying to grasp one chain of thought was proving to be rather more difficult than she thought possible. There had to be something she could do with the information. Should she tell Nico what she suspected? The real question was what did she want? Did she want to stop him from hurting anybody else? Or did she want to protect him?

She paced up and down. It took her six steps to get from one side of the room to the other. She ran her fingers through her hair and stopped mid-stride. She realised the only thing that mattered was the fact that she loved him. It didn't matter what he'd done. He was still the man she loved. And with this realisation all other choices flew out of the window.

*

After seeing Nico pack his box and walk out of the charge office, Louis didn't know what to do with himself. He had psyched himself up for today. He had all the answers ready for Nico; he'd been ready for him and now that Nico wasn't going to ask him any questions he felt deflated. It was as if he wasn't important enough to Nico: the women he'd killed and everything he'd done wasn't important.

He was going to show Nico that he was; he was going to make him realise he was the most important thing in Nico's life. He wasn't sure how he was going to achieve it. Thankfully he had the kind of job where all he had to do for long periods of time was to think. But thinking, he had discovered, wasn't always such a good thing.

Most of the day he'd spent parked under a tree but hadn't been able to come up with anything. All he had been able to think of was his fucking Bitch mother who was, thankfully, now burning in hell. With her out of the way he was in the clear. He'd circled around the thoughts swirling in his head for most of his shift. Then he would try to focus on showing Nico what was important but his thoughts kept returning to his mother lying in the mortuary waiting to be buried.

It was late when he arrived home and he still didn't have a fixed plan of action. He opened the front door to find Natalie pacing up and down the lounge with a smile spread across her face.

"What are you so happy about?" he asked her, finding it amusing to see her jump. He enjoyed giving her a fright and, being highly strung, she was an easy target. It didn't take much these days. It wasn't much of a challenge but it was still enjoyable.

"I didn't see you standing there," she said, pasting on another smile. "I was just thinking about our wedding. Speaking of which, I'd better give Janet a call. She's going to be my bridesmaid."

He was about to say something glib when he realised that Natalie had just given him a way to get back at Nico and secure his relationship with Natalie.

"I love you!" he shouted at her retreating back.

12

Friday, 19 July

It was a cold, overcast morning. Perfect weather for a funeral.

Louis had asked him to be one of the pall-bearers and now, with the weight of the coffin on his right shoulder, he wished he'd said no. At least he had a front row seat to the goings on and could watch both Louis and Natalie closely throughout the funeral. There were a total of ten people attending the funeral. The church was icy, with little body heat generated by the congregation; it was no surprise when he saw his own breath puffing out of his mouth every time he exhaled. If he hadn't already heard it from other sources, he would have the impression, from the low turnout, that Marietta Gouws was not a well-loved woman. Louis had asked four of the men he worked with to be pall-bearers. Louis, Nico and the other four pall-bearers carried the coffin to the front of the Methodist church and put it down in front of the pulpit. Janet was sitting next to Natalie and holding her hand. He didn't understand why Natalie needed to hold Janet's hand. It wasn't as though Natalie was broken up about Marietta Gouws's death.

Louis and Natalie, both dry-eyed, only showed some emotion when they thought they were being watched. Nico took his seat next to Janet and watched Louis make his way to the pulpit to give the eulogy. It was a beautiful speech but didn't quite correspond with what he had learned about the woman they were about to bury. It was possible that Louis could merely have been doing what most people did when a parent passed away. He'd found that people in general seemed to develop amnesia about the things the parents had done to them as children. They seemed to remember only the good things they had done and if there wasn't any good to remember, they made some up. Or, of course, Louis could be an excellent actor. He was more inclined to believe the latter.

After Louis's eulogy the pastor gave a long sermon. Only the hard, uncomfortable church pew kept Nico from falling asleep. That and the fact that he needed to stay vigilant to keep an eye on Louis. Nico shuffled from one butt cheek to another, trying to prevent his arse from going numb and swallowed a few yawns. Janet even poked him in the ribs a few times to wake him up.

Natalie stared straight ahead and nibbled on her fingertips and nails. She seemed to be listening to every word the pastor had to say. Louis sat relaxed on the wooden pew. How he managed to look so comfortable was a mystery. His right arm rested on the back of the pew and his hand on Natalie's shoulder, while his thumb stroked Natalie's shoulder, which she ignored.

The pastor finished his sermon and invited everyone to join them at the graveside for the burial. Nico heard Louis's four colleagues from work stand up behind him. Their footsteps echoed down the aisle and out of the church. The trolley to carry the coffin out of the church to the waiting hearse was wheeled in by funeral home attendants. He felt a tap on his shoulder. Louis was standing over him.

"It would mean a lot to us if you and Janet came with us to the graveside," Louis said to him.

Nico glanced sideways at Janet to see her reaction. She hugged Natalie around her shoulders and nodded her head.

"Sure," he said. "Not a problem."

"Thanks! I really do appreciate you coming today. Your support means a lot to me."

"I remember what it was like when my mother died. No one should have to go through this kind of thing alone." When the words came out he wanted to bite his tongue. Fucking hypocrite, he thought.

"Do you know how to get to the cemetery or do you want to follow us?"

"We'll follow you," Nico said. The drive there would give him time to think.

Nico's battered old Datsun stuttered as he started up the engine and backfired. It was at times like this that he missed having his police-issue Almera. Janet curled up on the passenger seat, her legs tucked in under her bum, leaving him to his jumbled thoughts. The drive to the Pretoria East cemetery was long and silent. Images swirled around in his head. His mind was a messy collage and the artist belonged in an insane asylum. He didn't know what to think or feel.

The tombstones looked forlorn under their blanket of weeds. Only a handful had flowers on them. People didn't come to cemeteries anymore. They weren't safe. A nun had been raped in the Irene cemetery a few months before. The rapist was still at large. Most people were now having family members cremated. It was safer. He couldn't help but wonder how many of these graves were ever visited by so-called loved ones. Then again, he was also guilty: he hadn't been to see his mother's grave in about five years. It was time he made an effort and paid her a visit, even if it was just to talk to a tombstone. And heaven help anyone who tried to mug him while he chatted to his long-dead mother. They walked deep into the cemetery, there were a few times when Nico thought they were lost.

Marietta Gouws's coffin was being lowered into her newly-dug grave as they arrived. The coffin descended slowly and made a thud as it hit the bottom of the grave. The gravediggers started shovelling earth onto the coffin. It hit the wood with a thud, scratching it. Some of the sand slid off the soft round edges and slipped to the side. Nico looked up from the partially-covered coffin and found Louis staring at Janet. The look in Louis's eyes set off those bells and this time he couldn't silence them. He looked at her the way a hungry predator stared at its prey. Cold fear rippled down his spine and sent a cold, nasty, tingly sensation through every nerve ending, making his fingers itch to reach across the grave a throttle the last breath out of Louis.

13

Two weeks had passed since the funeral and that uneasy feeling was still eating away at him. He had kept an eye on the papers but there wasn't a word about another body being left on display, floating in a bath tub. The Bathroom Strangler was already yesterday's news and had been replaced by a brutal family murder and yet another government scandal. A politician had been caught with his hand in the cookie jar, yet again, and a father had killed his wife and children with a hammer before sticking a knife in his own throat and bleeding to death. There were far easier ways of killing yourself, Nico thought while reading the Newspaper. Hadn't the man ever heard of using a gun? Government officials threatened to strike again. Nothing new there.

The Bathroom Strangler murders would slowly find their way into the pile of cold cases and then be added to the pile of unsolved cases. They would collect dust and fade from memory. Who besides the victims' families would care if the killer was caught or not? But in this case, the families in question didn't seem to care. The public was fickle and would embrace the next big scandal and forget about the Bathroom Strangler and his victims.

He crunched up the newspaper and threw it in the far corner of his lounge. The inactivity was getting to him. He needed to do something, but what? Laurel and Hardy had taken over the case and shoved it into some dusty corner and wouldn't listen to anything he had to say. A thought started to spark at the back of his mind and slowly took shape. He felt the synapses fire and play around his brain. Then a fully-fledged epiphany hit him right between his eyes. There was one person who probably knew the truth.

But he wasn't sure if she would speak to him.

*

It was early afternoon and things at the law firm where Natalie worked were in afternoon overdrive. Overdue urgent briefs were piled high on her desk. Dark hair fell over her face, touching her computer keyboard. She looked up at him through her hair as he approached her desk. Surprise, mingled with suspicion, marked her eyes, while her face remained expressionless.

"You busy?" Nico asked her.

She looked at the piles of paperwork on her desk, raised one eyebrow and looked back at him.

"Sorry, stupid question," he said before she could say anything.

"Don't take this the wrong way, but what are you doing here?"

"I just wanted to ask you some questions about Louis's mother."

"Why? I thought you'd been suspended."

"So you heard about that?"

"Bad news travels fast," she said, taking a piece of paper out of her printer and putting it into a red folder. The red folder was placed on top of another pile of folders in a paper tray marked Contracts. "What do you want to know about her?"

"Did she have any enemies, anyone who might have wanted her dead?"

"Anybody who knew her would fit that description."

"What was Louis's relationship like with his mother?"

"Excuse me?"

"Were Louis and his mother close?"

"What exactly are you driving at?" There was something in her tone that made him wonder even more about the relationship between mother and son.

"It's a simple question. Why are you being so defensive?" Had there been some kind of abuse?

"I'm not being defensive. I don't understand why you're asking me about Louis's relationship with that woman." The word *woman* seemed to stick in her throat.

"So I take it you two didn't get along?"

"You already know the answer to that one. Janet will doubtless have clued you in on all the sordid details."

"You caught me there."

"Look, Nico, Louis's mother and I were not on the best of terms. There's no secret there. As for Louis and his mother, well, their relationship was complicated."

"What do you mean by complicated?"

"That's all I can tell you right now. As you can see, I'm a very busy girl and if I don't get these out by the end of the day," she said, nodding her head at the pile of papers on her right, "you won't be the only one sitting at home."

"Thanks for your time, anyway. If you think of anything please give me a call."

"Don't worry, Nico. The moment I have anything else to say on the matter you'll be the first person I call."

He'd been dismissed.

He turned around at the door to Natalie's office and watched her typing as if her life depended upon the document she was working on. Her reaction to his questions had been strange and he knew he was on to something. Louis's relationship with his mother had been anything other than healthy.

The possibilities that came to mind made his stomach turn.

*

Nico's visit had taken her by surprise. Thinking back on it, as she stood in her kitchen after work and making coffee, she hadn't expected him to approach her. She didn't know what to do or how to act around Louis anymore. Now Nico was complicating everything. She loved Louis, even though she was afraid of him. Afraid of what he would do. She was also mad as all hell. She'd never allowed herself to be angry before. Fear, on the other hand, was something she was familiar with, anger was something new. She wasn't sure what she was supposed to do with all that rage she was feeling, boiling up inside her.

She poured the boiling water from the kettle into her chipped yellow coffee mug and looked up at the kitchen clock. Louis would be home soon. Since the funeral he had become increasingly irritable. Anything could set him off. He was probably suffering from withdrawal symptoms, she thought. Being on a five-week killing spree will do that to you. Not being able to take out his frustrations on his mother and all those women was obviously taking its toll. Sooner or later he would have to act on those frustrations again. He'd acquired a taste for it. She didn't want to be in the firing line when he went off.

She heard keys scraping against the lock. The sound of metal against metal brought back memories of being hand-cuffed to her steel-framed bed in the orphanage. The front door swung open and a man stood in the doorway. It took a few seconds for it to register that it was Louis and not the man from the orphanage. She managed to choke back a scream.

"What's with you?" he asked her.

"Nothing," she said, stirring her coffee with a shaky hand. The teaspoon connected with the cup a few too many times.

"*Ja*, right. That's why you've turned the mug and spoon into musical instruments."

"Whatever," she tapped the spoon against the rim of the mug. Excess droplets of coffee dripped off the spoon and down the side of the mug.

Louis made it across the kitchen in a few quick paces and grabbed her right upper arm. Coffee spilled over the edges of the mug, puddled around the base and slowly dribbled down the kitchen cabinet to the floor.

"What's your problem now?" she asked him. "Haven't you killed anyone lately?" She regretted the words the moment they left her mouth.

The back of Louis's hand connected with her cheek. The force of it pushed her back against the kitchen counter. Her back arched and her hand hit the coffee mug. The mug fell to the tiled floor and shattered into pieces. The spilt coffee pooled on the floor like blood. His hands were on her throat and tightened. His fingertips dug into her soft flesh around her windpipe.

"So you want to kill me too, like you did your mother?" Her voice was a hoarse whisper escaping with the last of her breath. His grip on her throat loosened. She fell to the floor and gasped for breath.

"I'm sorry. I'm so fucking sorry." He went down on his knees in front of her. "I love you. I could never ..."

"Get away from me," she hissed, kicking him and trying to scramble as close to the safety of the wall as possible.

"I don't know what came over me. I'm sorry," he said, as he stood up.

"I know what came over you, you sick murdering bastard!"

"Don't call me that. I did it all for you."

"That's such bullshit, you did it all for yourself. I didn't ask you to kill all those women. You killed them because you didn't have the balls to kill your mother sooner." She was on her feet and standing her ground without knowing how she came to be in that position.

He jerked his right hand back past his shoulder. She flinched. His hand dropped before it connected with her cheek.

"I'm not a coward," he said, as he walked towards the door.

"Are you going to kill some old woman again?"

"You'll see and just remember: you asked for this," he whispered before closing the door behind him.

Hysterical laughter echoed in the kitchen. It took a few minutes before Natalie realised that it was her own.

*

The next move he planned would kill two birds with one stone. He would teach Natalie and Nico a harsh lesson in manners. It would be one they would never forget. A slow smile crept along his lips as he knocked on her door. The light above the door was out. Luck was with him tonight. Even if someone saw him go in they would never be able to give a decent description. The pot plants outside her door needed water and were starting to wilt. She'd never been much of a gardener. The wind howled through the passage and rustled the leaves of her plants. He pushed his hands deeper into his pockets.

"Shit, it's cold out here," he grumbled to himself. "What's taking the whore so long? She never used to be so slow."

He checked his watch: it was just after seven. He was cutting it fine, but it was worth the risk. He had to make sure that Nico would be here at just the right moment. She should be here he thought, as he knocked again and tapped his foot on the ground. He knocked again, harder this time. Her car was parked downstairs in its usual spot; he had made sure of that. Footsteps made their way to the front door. The lock jingled as the key was turned from the inside. The door opened as far as the security chain would allow it. She peered around the edge of the door and looked at him in surprise.

"What are you doing here?" Janet asked. "I thought we agreed when Natalie had her ... accident that we wouldn't see each other anymore." She stammered like the guilty bitch she was. "What we had was great but we agreed to stay away from each other for her sake."

"You mean you decided that we should stop. That's not why I'm here. We need to talk and it's windy out here, so if you don't mind, can I please come in?" he asked shoving his hands deeper into his jacket pockets.

"Oh, sorry," she said, closing the door. The security chain slid out and the door opened once again. "Look, this is a bad time. Nico's going to be here any moment." She opened the door wider. "He'll have questions if he sees you here."

"I just wanted to get your advice on something. I won't be here that long," he said as he stepped inside.

The door closed behind him. The familiar feel of the wire scraping against the fake leather of his gloves brought back the pleasant tingle he always felt at these moments. Her life was in his hands. This is what god must feel like when he takes someone's life, he thought.

"What do you need my advice about?" she asked, walking

past him into her lounge. "Has it got something to do with Nats?"

He pulled the wire out of his pocket, careful not to make any sudden movements. He wanted to give her the surprise of her life. The curve of her neck enticed him. She'd always loved it when he kissed her neck. She was two steps ahead of him. He closed the gap before she reached the couch. He crossed his wrists and flipped the wire over her head.

"What the ..." were the only words that escaped from her lips.

He jerked the wire through her throat, hard and fast, slicing the carotid artery. Blood flowed like a rich burgundy wine out of her throat and ran down the front of her white knitted jersey, turning it pink. Her body fell to the floor and her blood seeped into her clean beige carpet. It was over too quickly for him. He had wanted to savour the moment, the way he had always enjoyed their games before. She had been willing to do the things that Natalie wouldn't and then had the nerve to look down on him. He had wanted to make her suffer, to watch her squirm. He knelt over her body and turned her over. Her lifeless face, which had always taunted him in bed then rejected him once she'd had her fill, stared back at him. His fists crushed into her face over and over again. Each time his fist connected with her face he became more aroused.

The climax that had eluded him while he slit her throat exploded in his pants.

*

Nico was late for their date. Janet had invited him over for a romantic dinner. This probably meant she had ordered take-out from the Chinese Restaurant around the corner. Janet did not believe in cooking: that's why take-out restaurants existed. He took the stairs two at a time up to her second floor flat and was breathing heavily by the time he reached the landing.

"That's taken care of my exercise for the rest of the month," he said as he huffed his way towards her door.

The door was ajar. Janet was security conscious and never forgot to lock it, let alone close it properly. In fact, she always had the security chain hooked in place. A feeling of dread started to seep into his bones. He removed his Berretta from his ankle holster and pushed the door open with the toe of his shoe. His heart pounded. If anything happened to Janet he wouldn't be able to handle it. With his back against the door, he entered Janet's small, dark hallway. The back of his shirt scraped along the rough wall as he made his way down the unlit passage. The open kitchen door was on his right. He crouched down on his haunches and peered around the kitchen door. The light from the hallway outside shone in through the window giving the kitchen an atmosphere of foreboding. It was strange and made everything look as though it was trapped in time. The objects in the kitchen had no definition, no body. It was as though they would disappear if he blinked. White plastic bags stood on the kitchen counter. A box from the Chinese Restaurant stood next to the bags. The red dragon emblem emblazoned across the front of the white box containing what was to have been his dinner.

He closed his eyes and tried to convince himself that Janet was fine. That she would walk through the front door and ask him what exactly he thought he was doing crouching in the dark. She would see his pistol gripped tightly in his hands; she would raise her eyebrow; she would shake her head at him and tell him to put the damn thing away. She didn't like guns. He opened his eyes but Janet wasn't there. Somewhere deep inside him a voice told him that she would never walk through that door again. He made his way quietly through her flat, careful not to alert anybody to his presence should there still be someone lurking, waiting for him.

It was in the lounge that his fears were confirmed. The moon shone though the window showing off the contrast between the rough carpet and the smooth surface of a puddle of liquid in the middle of the floor. In the darkness he couldn't make out what it was. His gut and experience told him that it was blood but he prayed Janet had spilled a bottle of wine and hadn't had a chance to clean it up yet. Quietly, he made his way to the centre of the room and the puddle. He dipped his right index finger into it and smelt the distinctive coppery tang. His heart lurched and blood pounded in his ears. There was no doubt in his mind. It was blood: very fresh blood. The trail of blood led out of the lounge and down the passage towards her bedroom and bathroom. Watching where he placed his feet, he followed the trail that was seeping into her carpets.

He paused at her bedroom door and forced himself to survey the whole room. Everything was still in its place. The bed was still made. Janet never could bring herself to leave home without making her bed. She even insisted on making his bed whenever she spent the night. He had laughed and teased her about it. He called it her bed fetish. The stream of blood lead into her en suite bathroom. The wrenching in his gut told him what he would find in the bath. It was an all too familiar scene. Stumbling over his feet, he dragged himself across the room towards the bathroom.

The same light that illuminated the kitchen shone in through the high bathroom window. He stood at the door. Fear froze him in time. He had no sense of how long it took him to take in the bloody scene in front of him. It seemed to take forever to raise his eyes from the tiled floor to the bath. The light from outside illuminated what was left of Janet's face. Water, dyed red from her blood, ran over the edge of the bath and dripped onto the white tiles. Sinking to his knees, he rocked backwards and forwards mumbling incoherent words. Tears streamed down his face.

It took an hour before his brain started to work again and he realised that he had to report the fact that the love of his life had been murdered by the man he had failed to bring to justice. Once his mind started to work again, he fumbled in his jeans' pocket and pulled out his cell phone. The cell phone's screen lit up with a green glow. Staring down at the luminous screen he tried to remember what number he was supposed to be dialling. After what seemed an eternity, he managed to make his shaking fingers cooperate and dial Pete's number.

*

Louis sat in his car parked on the corner across from Janet's block of flats. He rubbed his raw knuckles as he waited. They reminded him of the beating he'd given that two-faced slut. He watched Nico arrive in his old Datsun *bakkie*. A smile had played on his lips as he imagined what Nico's reaction would be to finding Janet's body floating in her bathtub. He could see the water turning red with her blood. Looking at the photo's he'd taken on his digital camera gave him a rush all over again. If only he could have taken a photo of Nico's reaction. His cock was rock hard and strained against his jeans.

He wondered if Nico would cry or get angry and break things. The idea of solid Nico losing his mind was entertaining. Would the tragedy of losing his girlfriend drive him over the edge? The idea made him laugh out loud. It was a strange, almost hysterical, laughter that seemed to reverberate around the confined space of his Golf.

An hour and a half passed while he waited for the show to start. Must have been a slow night. It normally took the cops a lot longer to show up, if they showed up at all. He'd heard of cases where it took them more than two hours to arrive on a scene. But if the cops were doing their jobs, he and other security guys would be out of jobs. A police car careered around the corner on two wheels and squealed to a halt in front of her block, followed closely by an unmarked police car. A man wearing a pair of wrinkled black pants and old well-worn Adidas sneakers got out of the unmarked police vehicle and walked through the front entrance followed by other policemen in uniform. Louis recognised him as the man who worked closely with Nico. He struggled to remember his name. There were several articles in the Pretoria News that mentioned both Nico and the new arrival. The name sat on the tip of his tongue. He felt it tugging at the back of his mind.

"Fuck it! What is his name?" he asked himself out loud and smacked his palm against the steering wheel.

While he struggled to remember the man's name, another car pulled up and Laurel and Hardy got out and followed the others inside.

"Dr fucking Papenfuss," he said and smacked the steering wheel once again. "I knew I recognised that fucking piece of shit."

The arrival of the police cars on the scene made his heart pound. The adrenalin that had rushed through his veins while he killed Janet started to flow once again. It was the kind of high that no drugs could emulate. The crime scene vehicle arrived. It was a white truck with a single blue line in the middle of it. The arrival of all the players meant it was time for him to go. That black photographer would be out any moment to take photos of the area and of the faces in the crowd. As much as he wanted to stay and watch the show, he couldn't risk being seen. He reversed out of his parking spot under the trees and drove away slowly. There was no need to rush.

14

Pete stood in the doorway. The light from the hallway illuminated his tall crumpled figure from behind. The light gave him the appearance of having a bright yellow and white aura surrounding him, making him larger than life. Then again, Nico admitted to himself, in his present state of mind anything appeared to be bigger than life. He saw everything through a haze and the world moved in slow motion. This must be what they call an out-of-body experience he decided. It felt surreal, as though he were watching it all through someone else's eyes. He watched Pete walk, in slow motion, over to where he was crouched, leaning against the wall opposite the front door. The touch of Pete's hand on his shoulder made him shudder.

"Are you all right?" Pete's voice was low and sounded muffled to Nico's ears. Somewhere down the road a dog barked. Nico felt himself drift away. He didn't want to feel the pain. He wanted Janet to stand up and get out of her bathtub and tell him that everything was okay. He could almost see her smiling at him.

"Nico, are you all right?" Pete asked again, with the patience that only someone who has seen pain and tragedy too many times in his lifetime can summon.

Nico felt Pete's hand on his shoulder apply pressure and his voice brought him back into his own body. Janet's smiling face faded into the darkness and was replaced by Pete's worried face. The reality of Janet's death hit him hard. Bile rose up from his empty stomach. He stumbled up on to his feet and staggered past Pete, out of the door and managed to get his head over the railing, where the little that had been in his stomach made its way out with full force.

"At least you remembered the integrity of the crime scene. I just hope no one was walking past downstairs."

"Not now, Doc." It was all Nico could manage to get out between heaves.

"I'm sorry. Bad timing," he said, while patting Nico on his back. "Are you going to be okay to answer some questions?"

Nico nodded, crouched down on his haunches and gripped on to the railing.

"I'll answer any questions you have but I'll never be okay again." His voice croaked as he struggled to utter a coherent sentence.

Heavy footsteps walked up to them. They stopped a few steps away. He glanced under his arm to see who the new arrivals were. He noticed the well-worn brown shoes first, on both pairs of feet, then one pair of skinny legs and one pair of well-rounded legs. One pair of slacks was perfectly ironed and the other he doubted had ever seen an iron. He looked up at the faces for confirmation. Laurel and Hardy stared back at him with expressions he couldn't read. Laurel shuffled his feet and Hardy coughed. Both dropped their eyes, unable to meet Nico's anguished stare.

"Don't you have a crime scene to walk?" Pete asked them.

"We're waiting for you," was Hardy's response.

"I'll be with you in a moment. So get to work while I get a statement from the Captain, or do you have a problem with that?"

"No, no problem at all. But we want the Captain to join us at the station after we're through here."

"What for?" Pete's face started turning red as he asked Hardy. Nico had only seen his face go that red once before. It had been during Pete's divorce and his soon-to-be-ex-wife had been on the receiving end. He couldn't remember the reason; Pete's ex-wife just had to walk into the room for him to be angry. There were only two people who could get that kind of reaction out of the doctor: Hardy and his ex-wife.

"We're just covering all our bases. We just want to get a complete statement from the Captain at the station. That's all, or do you have a problem with that, Doctor?"

"Me? Have a problem with the two of you? Perish the thought."

"Look, Doctor, we know that you have a man crush on wonder boy over there, busy puking his guts out. We don't really want to know the details of your relationship, but we would however appreciate some cooperation from you while we work this case. Can you do that?" Laurel said, getting his two cents in.

"Don't get cute with me, Colonel. Now, before we turn this crime scene into a triple homicide I suggest we all get back to work." He turned to Nico, his voice losing the edge it had when talking to Laurel and Hardy and asked, "Do you think you can work the scene with us?"

Nico felt his stomach tighten again and his face must have betrayed his feelings.

"That's against procedure. Captain Van Staaden has been suspended," Hardy said, his voice two octaves higher than usual.

"I'm sorry, but I need your input on this," Pete said, ignoring Hardy. He couldn't meet Nico's eyes and his voice took on a pleading quality. "You knew her better then anybody else. We need you. Hell ... Janet needs you to pull yourself together and help us find the guy who did this to her."

"You're not playing fair, Doc," Nico mumbled.

"Do you think this fucker is going to play fair and stick to the rules? Can you trust these two idiots to do your job for you?" Pete asked, jutting his thumb in the direction of Laurel and Hardy.

"Who are you calling idiots?" Laurel and Hardy asked in unison.

"Would you all just shut up and stop your shit. A woman, who I loved , has just been murdered," Nico said, as he pulled himself up using the railing. "The longer we stand out here and argue, the longer her body deteriorates and the more evidence we lose. So, is it asking too much for you pathetic excuses for human beings to put your problems aside and fucking-well do your jobs?"

A slow triumphant smile crept on to Pete's face. "So ... does this mean you'll work the scene with me?"

"Wipe that smile off your face and I will, but we're missing a photographer."

"No, you're not," replied a voice whose body was hidden behind Laurel and Hardy.

"Thabiso, where the hell have you been?" asked Pete as

Thabiso's head emerged from between the shoulders of Laurel and Hardy.

"I've been here the whole time. I didn't want to interrupt the cock fight."

"Well, now that everybody is present and accounted for, can we please just get this over and done with?" Nico could feel his resolve starting to crumble. He wanted to run and hide. He still wanted some one to knock him out so that when he woke up, Janet would be standing over him, alive and well.

Nico followed Thabiso into Janet's flat. Pete instructed Laurel and Hardy to wait outside and told them that they could have the scene once he was finished. Laurel and Hardy threatened to report him to Molwedi. Nico didn't pay any attention to the rest of the insults being flung around; all he could see was Janet's blood on her clean carpet. Bile rose up from his now-raw gut. Thabiso's camera flashed, illuminating the dark room. The room spun around him. A hand steadied him and he could breathe again. The air smelt of blood, Janet's blood. It mingled with the fragrance of her perfume. It was a strangely sweet smell which made him feel the loss of her even more keenly.

Tears flowed down his cheeks. He hadn't cried since his mother's funeral and hadn't thought he'd ever cry again. This wasn't the way things were supposed to be. He'd had a picture of his life with Janet, of what their wedding would be like, of what their children would look like. He'd imagined that they'd look like their mother.

He looked around at Janet's flat, at where she'd died and those dreams of their future together evaporated.

There was no sign of struggle. Nothing had been overturned. All her ornaments were still perfectly displayed, just the way she always insisted on having them. Nothing was out of place.

"Looks like he caught her by surprise," Pete said; he seemed to be reading Nico's mind as always. "My guess is she knew the guy. What do you think van Staaden?"

Nico only managed to nod his head. He couldn't think. The walls were closing in on him.

They walked from the lounge down the passage into her bedroom. Seeing her bed with the clean white sheets brought back painful memories of falling asleep to the sound of her breathing, her blonde hair strewn across the pillow and creamy-white eye lids fluttering as she dreamed. He remembered lying awake next to her, watching her sleep, guarding her. The failure of unspoken promises hit him hard. He felt as though he had been driven over by a bulldozer and the bulldozer was reversing for another shot at him. Each memory hit him harder than the last one. Each hit from the bulldozer sent him spiralling into another memory. He felt a hand guide him out of the bedroom and into hell.

"Overkill," Pete muttered to himself as he leaned over Janet's body. "Our boy was a tad frustrated and worked it out on your girl. I'd say she was already dead when he beat her face to a pulp."

The sight of her body floating in the bathtub, suspended in time, brought him out of the whirling memories. Reality hit him with a force he hadn't felt since he found his mother's body. At that moment he hated Pete for making him go though that. It was cruel.

"Oh, god! I can't do this. Not again." Blood pounded in his ears in time with his feet as he ran out of the bathroom. The light from the corridor blinded his eyes as he emerged from the darkness of Janet's tomb. He shielded them from the glaring brightness of the lights and the flashes from press photographers who somehow had wind of another murder.

He heard a voice calling his name; it sounded as though it was coming from afar. For all he knew it was from another world. He looked, unseeing, in the direction of the voice. Another flash from a camera distorted his vision. Through a haze of spots in front of his eyes he could see a woman standing in the crowd trying to attract his attention. For a few seconds he thought it might be Janet. His vision cleared and he recognised the woman. It was Helen. He had loved her almost as much as he loved Janet. He would never understand why she had betrayed him for the sake of her career. He would never have chosen his job over the person he loved.

Her suit was tailored and looked expensive. Her hair was the same blonde as Janet's, but hers was long, straight and sleek. So unlike Janet's short wavy hairstyle that she said made her look like a young Meg Ryan. Helen always managed to look composed and serene when everything around her was in chaos, whereas Janet was always flustered but tried so hard to control things going on around her. They looked so much alike, but were so different. He tried to ignore Helen's insistent voice. She was the last person he wanted to deal with right now. He turned his back on her and ended up facing Laurel and Hardy's sour faces. Their eyes judged him. He changed his mind. Laurel and Hardy were the last people he wanted to deal with.

He turned around once more and tried to find somewhere to hide from Helen, as well as everybody else's accusing eyes. Helen had moved her way forward, dragging her cameraman with her. She was now pushing against the yellow crime-scene tape and arguing with a constable who was trying to get her to stand back and pushing the camera out of his face only to find the microphone where the camera had been. She'd always been pushy. Up until now he'd managed to avoid her and other journalists since their break up but now he was her main target. She smelt blood and would go in for the kill. She always did. It made her good at her job, but a lousy human being.

*

The interrogation room was cold and the atmosphere hostile. The overhead bulb didn't give off much light. The shadows played like ghosts in the corners of the room. It was the first time he had been on this side of the desk. The plastic chair was uncomfortable and he felt as though it was going to collapse beneath him at any moment. The air was heavy with the smell of bad body odour. Pete came in with two cups of coffee and placed one in front of Nico. He removed a pack of

Camel's from his jacket pocket and offered one to Nico. Nico took one without thinking and put it between his lips. Not noticing where the match came from, he inhaled deeply. The nicotine felt good as it entered his exhausted body.

"Have there been any new developments on the case?" Nico asked Pete, after taking a sip of his hot, black coffee.

"Not until now."

Nico took a deep drag from his cigarette and exhaled slowly.

"I see," he said, squinting across the dimly-lit room at Pete who had retreated into a corner on the other side of the room. "Can you please tell me why not?"

"You know I can't, and besides you know the answer to that one already."

"True. No leads, no case. It just ended up at the bottom of the pile and now that he's killed Janet, the wheels are moving again."

Pete touched the tip of his nose with his index finger and nodded his head.

"There's just one problem," Nico continued. "Janet doesn't fit the victim profile and she wasn't killed on a Sunday."

"That's correct. So you aren't such an idiot after all."

"And I bet no one's looked into Louis Gouws?"

"Nope. Laurel and Hardy felt he didn't have enough of a motive and didn't fit the profile. Plus his girlfriend gave him an alibi for all the murders."

"You have got to be kidding me: he fits the profile to a fucking T. And Natalie's lying. She wasn't with him those nights. I'm telling you – he's our guy. What about the missing wire in his mother's piano? Did they just forget about that?"

"They're incompetent idiots. I don't think they even bothered to follow up."

"I just can't shake the feeling that he's ..." He was interrupted by the door opening. Laurel and Hardy walked in.

They both had smug grins on their faces. If he were a betting man, he would have bet a month's salary that they had wanted to put him through hell for quite some time and they were going to enjoy this opportunity. The thought that they were deriving pleasure from his misery made his skin crawl. He refused to let them break him. Who the hell did they think they were? Did they think they could just waltz in and take advantage of his tragedy.

"So, Van Staaden," Hardy said as he pulled a chair out from under the desk and parked his ample rear. He pressed 'record' on the tape recorder in front of Nico. It was the first time Nico had noticed it was in front of him. "Do you want to tell us about your relationship with the deceased?"

"Not particularly, no. Besides you know exactly what my relationship with her was." Nico said, trying to keep the anger out of his voice. He didn't want to give them the satisfaction of rattling him.

"Van Staaden, there's no need to be defensive," Laurel said, sitting next to Hardy and picking at his fingers. He seemed to be bored by the proceedings.

"I'm not being defensive." Then he turned to Pete and asked. "Am I being defensive?"

"I don't think so. He asked a stupid question," Pete replied, examining his fingernails and deciding that they needed to be cleaned, he removed his penknife from his shirt pocket and proceeded to clean his finger nails.

"Doctor, you know as well as I do that we need to establish the relationship between the deceased and Captain van Staaden for the record," said Hardy turning around in his chair and facing Pete, who shrugged his shoulders in reply. Hardy turned back to Nico and took a deep breath.

"Captain van Staaden, would you state, for the record, the nature of your relationship with the deceased?"

"She was my girlfriend." The words came with difficulty and reminded him that she was gone. Antagonising Laurel and Hardy provided him with a brief respite from reality but having to talk about her, to these men who delighted in his grief, brought him back to the reason for him being in this small, dark room and he remembered that Janet was lying on a slab in the mortuary, with her throat slit.

"Van Staaden! Are you still with us?" Laurel's voice interrupted his thoughts.

"Umm, sorry." His voice sounded hollow to his own ears.

"So you and the deceased were involved intimately?" Hardy asked

"Isn't that what I just said and her name was Janet Shaw, not the deceased or the victim. Her name was Janet Shaw. For fuck's sake, what is wrong with you people? She was a human being, not some piece of meat. She had a name."

"Calm down, Captain."

"I will not calm down. I lost someone very important to me and you're acting like she was nothing, like she was just another victim."

His hands were shaking as he took another drag from his cigarette. Pete appeared at his side and squatted down on his haunches.

"Calm down, Nico. These arseholes want to see you lose it," he said in a low voice. "Don't let them get to you."

"Hey, who the hell are you calling an arsehole?" Hardy asked, his paunch leaning against the rickety table as he leaned forward to hear what Pete was saying.

"That would be you," Pete said. "Now drag your gut off the table before you break it." He turned back to Nico.

"Watch your step, Doctor, or you'll find yourself sitting outside," Hardy said, his face turning red.

"I need you on this." Pete ignored Hardy. "I need you to keep your head. Can you do that for me?"

Nico nodded his head and with shaky hands took his cigarette to his lips for another, long, drag.

"To you, Janet's not just another victim but to everybody else, she is. She also needs you to keep calm and keep cool. Okay?"

"I'm okay, Doc. You don't need to give me another pep talk. I'll be fine. I just want to get this over with, so I can get out there and find this bastard."

"You won't be getting anybody," Hardy said with a glint in his eyes that Nico realised was pure pleasure. The bastard was really enjoying this.

"What do you mean I won't be getting anybody?"

"In case you've forgotten, Molwedi threw you off the case,"

Laurel said and smiled. "Oh yes, I almost forgot … you're also suspended. And here's the real kicker … we don't think your girlfriend was killed by the Bathroom Strangler."

"What the fuck?" Nico turned to look at Pete, who was examining his shoes. "Doc?"

Pete took a deep breath before answering.

"Look, Nico, the fact is, she doesn't fit the victim profile, which you also stated. Plus the severe beating and it wasn't a Sunday. This could be a copycat killing."

"You're kidding me, right?"

"You see, van Staaden, this is what we think happened." Hardy bristled with excitement. "We think you got there when she was still very much alive. You got into a fight which turned really nasty. Am I getting warm, Captain?"

"I don't believe this." The realisation that they thought he'd killed Janet felt like a million knives slicing into him. "Doc, please tell me you aren't buying this load of crap?"

"You know I don't but it's out of my hands. You're not the only one off the case. I crashed this party."

"You're off the case?"

"Yes."

"When did that happen?"

"About twenty minutes ago."

"Sorry to interrupt your little discussion, but Doctor, you have overstayed your welcome," Laurel said, obviously relishing the situation.

"Fine, I'll leave."

"No! Wait a minute, Doc," Nico said, standing up. "Are you arresting me?" he asked, looking at Hardy.

"We're just having a little chat, Captain."

"Well, since you're not arresting me I'll be leaving too, then." He pulled his jacket on and turned to Pete. "You coming, Doc?"

"Right behind you."

"Van Staaden," Hardy said as they reached the door. "Don't leave town."

"You know," Nico said, smiling for the first time in hours. "You watch too much TV."

15

Leaning against the white TV van and squinting at the entrance to the police station, across the road, Helen watched him walk out of the main entrance. The light above the door illuminated his scowling face. Her reporter's nose told her something was happening and she had to know about it. Helen's cameraman, Kyle, was sitting enjoying his coffee in the driver's seat.

"Hey, Kyle, grab the camera," Helen instructed.

"Why?" he asked, startled, trying not to spit his coffee out all over the dashboard.

"Because I said so; Captain van Staaden and Dr. Papenfuss have just walked out, looking seriously unhappy."

"What did you expect? The dude just lost his girlfriend."

"I know that. I may be blonde but I'm not stupid," she said, flicking her hair over her shoulder. "There's something else going on. Now stop messing around and get your arse in gear."

"Yes, ma'am." He picked up the camera from the seat next to him and slid out of the van.

They ran across the road, dodging cars, while Kyle's camera bounced against his thigh. Headlights from the oncoming cars flashed at them. They reached Nico and Pete, who were standing next to Nico's Datsun, just as Nico was about to unlock his car door. Kyle's camera was hoisted on to his shoulder and placed strategically in front of Nico's face. Helen, holding her microphone as though it was an extension of her arm, placed herself to the right of Kyle and his camera, so that he could pan between her and Nico easily and still be able to get a shot of Pete.

"Captain van Staaden, could we just ask you a few questions?" she said, placing the microphone in front of him. She was always the professional journalist no matter what her personal involvement. Nico had never been able to understand that about her.

"No comment," Nico said and opened his door.

He always was a cold bastard when cornered, she thought.

"Fuck off with that camera," Pete said, while putting his hand in front of the camera and pushing it out of the way.

"Hey, that's expensive equipment," Kyle said, moving his camera out of the way of Pete's large hands. He held the camera down next to his thigh with the lens tilted upwards so that he could still film and covered the red recording light with his thumb. "Relax the camera's off."

"It better be," Pete said, standing with his legs slightly apart, pointing an angry finger at Kyle.

"At least talk to me off the record." Helen tried for her sincerest smile.

"Why on earth would I talk to you, on or off the record?"

"Because whether you talk to me or not, you are going to be headline news. If you talk to me you get your side of the story across. If you don't ... well, then you can't blame me if you get crucified on the news. Nico, I still care about you. That hasn't changed and I can't bear to see you like this. Please let me be here for you. Let me help you," she pleaded.

"Helen, you are incapable of caring for anybody except yourself and right now I couldn't care less about what you people have to say about me. I have probably lost my job, my girlfriend is dead and I'm officially the main suspect in her murder," he said, getting into his car. As he turned the key in the ignition, he turned to her and looked straight into Kyle's camera and said, "Now you have your footage for the late news." He closed the car door.

Helen watched him drive off. Pete was blustering about the freedom of the press being the eleventh plague on humanity and that the Media Tribunal wasn't such a bad idea after all, if it meant putting a muzzle on overly zealous journalists who didn't practice due diligence.

"Would you shut up," she said turning to Pete. "I'm trying to think."

"What are you cooking up in that scheming little brain of yours?" Kyle asked.

"What do you mean little?"

"A tad sensitive this evening, aren't we?"

"Oh, shut up and come with me," she said, as she shoved her microphone at Kyle, and strutted back towards the van.

"How do you work with that bitch?" Pete asked Kyle, who was staring after Helen and shaking his head.

"She's not that bad. She just has a job to do and you guys don't exactly make it easy for her. That pisses her off. She's funny that way."

"Let me guess," Pete said. "You're screwing her?"

"What?" Kyle stammered. "What makes you say that?"

"Are you coming, Kyle?" Helen yelled before Pete could answer. She reached the road and was tapping her foot in a quick staccato.

"Yeah, I'm coming," he said and trotted off after her like a faithful puppy who knew he was about to get smacked with the newspaper, but went anyway in the hope that he'd get a treat instead of a smack on the nose.

"So ..." he said once back inside the van. "What's going on?"

"How do you feel about clearing an innocent man of murder, finding the real killer and winning the CNN African Journalist of the year award?"

"Interesting idea; bloody difficult, if not down right impossible but an interesting idea none the less," he said, patting himself down to find his pack of smokes. "Any idea as to how we're going to do this?"

"Well ... knowing Nico ... he'll do all the work for us. No matter what he says, he'll call me when he needs me and then all we need to do is show up with the camera and the right spin."

*

Natalie lay back in the hot bath watching the steam rise in wisps around her. This was her thinking time. Louis was working the night shift; at least she hoped that was what he was doing. So, she was alone for the night. The sound of Vanessa Mae playing her violin drifted through the flat. She needed the music to calm her frazzled nerves. Now that his mother wasn't there to blame, he was using her as punching bag even more than normal and blaming her for Nico's absence since the funeral. He also blamed Janet for their problems and every time Louis hit her he said it was Janet's fault. It was Janet's influence on her that made her taunt and defy him. His rants were confused and belligerent. Janet wasn't their problem. He was.

"What am I going to do?" she asked herself as she slid under the bath water. She breathed out slowly, enjoying the sound of her breathing under the water. The water was warm and comforting. She felt safe.

The burning candles looked like strange fairy dancers from beneath the water. She heard her bubbles of breath breaking on the surface. Her lungs tightened as they ran out of air, but she ignored it and stayed under until her lungs felt as though they were going to collapse. She came up fast and gasped in all the air her starved lungs could take. The candle flames objected to the sudden disturbance to their air supply and threatened to stop their dance. She leaned back and rested her head against the tiled wall behind her. The enamel of the bath above the water level felt cold against her hot skin.

The intercom buzzing made her jump and water dribbled over the edge onto the white tiles of the bathroom floor.

"Who the hell?" she said under her breath, as she climbed out of the bath and wrapped a small towel around her thin frame. The intercom kept buzzing. She slid her wet feet into her fluffy slippers and trudged out of the steamy bathroom into the cold passageway.

"Hello," she answered the incessant buzzing.

"It's me," answered Nico's voice.

"Louis's not here."

"I know. I'm here to see you."

"Here we go," she said to herself as she buzzed him in, noticing that the towel only just covered her in the right places. She wondered if she had time to put anything else on. The knock came before she could make up her mind and ended up answering the door with the towel on the verge of falling around her feet.

The expression on his face was not what she had expected. His eyes were bloodshot and puffy. He looked as if he'd been crying for hours. This was not good, she decided. Something was terribly wrong.

"Are you all right?" she asked, as he walked past her into the lounge area.

"I'll just go and put on some clothes while you make yourself comfortable," she said, when he didn't answer her. He just stared at her but somehow she had the impression that he didn't really see her. She came back wearing a black pair of tracksuit pants and one of Louis's jerseys. Sitting down opposite him she waited for him to say something.

After a few minutes the silence started to get the better of her nerves.

"Okay Nico, this is driving me nuts. Would you please tell me what's going on?" She stood up and started pacing. Nico said nothing. "Is it Janet? Is she all right?"

Nico raised his bloodshot eyes to meet hers. Something in his pain-filled eyes told her that her suspicion was correct .

"No, it can't be." She collapsed on the couch. "I spoke to her yesterday."

"She was killed a few hours ago." His voice sounded hollow and as dead as Janet.

"No, I don't believe you. Is this some kind of sick joke?" Tears streamed down her face. She knew he was telling her the truth but she couldn't bring herself to believe it.

"If you don't believe me, maybe you should ask Louis. I'm sure he would be able to go into great detail of how she died."

"No, he wouldn't have … You're lying."

"Wouldn't have what, Natalie? Killed her the way he did his mother and all those other women?" He shook his head. "Why would I lie to you?"

She didn't have an answer for him. She didn't know why she was so shocked. Deep down she'd known this was coming but now that it had it was a shock.

The truth hit her in the stomach and she doubled over with grief and pain. He had killed the only person who mattered to her. The only person who kept her from taking that plunge over the edge of sanity was gone. He had dealt the cruellest blow possible. She heard a strange discordance, like someone strangling a cat. It took a few seconds before she realised that she was the one making the sound. She dropped to the floor and Nico stood over her. Disgust and pity mingled in his eyes.

"How does it make you feel knowing that you're responsible for the death of the only person who gave a shit about you?" he hissed at her.

"I didn't have anything to do with her death. It's not my fault," she said but couldn't help but wonder if he was right. Was it her fault?

"That's right: just keep telling yourself that. You could have prevented this. You knew he was a monster but did nothing. You protected him."

"You're lying. He's not a monster and he wouldn't have killed her. He loves me. He wouldn't do that to me or to Janet." She crawled away from him, tears burning their way down her cheeks. "You're wrong. You have to be wrong," she whispered.

"You might have fooled Janet with your little-miss-victim routine, but you aren't fooling me. The only reason you're upset she's dead is because you didn't see it coming. You didn't see the writing on the wall. You can't control him. He's not some pet, Natalie. He's a wild animal and he's turned on you." His words stung. Each word was a punch to her stomach, sending her reeling.

"No, you're wrong. I loved her and so did he. Louis wouldn't do that to her any more than he would do that to me. We were a family. The three of us."

"Oh please, you wouldn't know what love is if it smacked you in the face. And he *did* do this to her and he *will* do the same thing to you."

"I loved her." She felt the wall against her back. There wasn't anywhere for her to run. She was trapped.

"Prove it." His face was inches from hers. She smelt beer and cigarettes.

"What?"

"It's your fault she's dead. You could have stopped him from killing again but you didn't. I don't know why and right now I don't really care. The fact is Janet is dead and you let it happen." He was standing over her again, then started to pace up and down in front of her. She felt as though he was prowling around his prey. She didn't like being anybody's prey. He was circling, waiting to attack.

She tried to prepare herself for what came next, but how can one prepare for the onslaught that comes from someone's deep seated grief, when they have nothing left to lose. . He dragged her to her feet and slammed her against the wall.

"You fucking-psycho-bitch." Drops of spittle hit her face. "Give me one good reason why I shouldn't put your sorry arse in prison for the rest of your life."

"Because I didn't commit a crime and you need me," her voice was hoarse and it escaped in a whisper.

"I need you?" he shouted and let her drop back to the floor. "Why do I need you?"

"We both know you really want to punish Louis, not me," her voice was soft and stroking.

"Oh, trust me, I want to punish you but lucky for you, Louis's the one I need to stop right now."

"And I can help you do that." She walked up to him and put her hand on his shoulder. "Please let me help you. Let me do this for Janet."

She felt his body shake beneath her hand. At first she thought he was crying, then he tilted his head back and he started to laugh. Her hand jerked off his shoulder.

"Oh, you *are* going to help me, Natalie." He stopped laughing and turned to face her.

"What do you want me to do?"

"First go and pack a bag for a few days. Louis is going to get a bit of a surprise when he comes home."

16

The light above the door was out, which Louis found strange – he had replaced the bulb two days ago – and the door was ajar. Natalie always locked it. His heart pounded in his chest. He kicked the door open. It banged against the wall and bounced back towards him.

"Natalie," he called from the doorway.

Silence.

"Natalie," he called again, this time louder. His voice reached a higher pitch than usual and squeaked like a thirteen-year-old boy whose voice was breaking.

He heard the wind howl through an open window in the kitchen. The kitchen curtains flapped and disturbed the leaves of her herbs on the window sill. He took a tentative step inside and stood in the hallway.

"What the fuck is she up to now?" he mumbled under his breath.

There were more dangerous predators in Pretoria than him. He only hoped that nothing had happened to her. She was trying to teach him a lesson or it was one of her other stupid games. He didn't know what he would do if anything happened to her. What if she tried to kill herself again? The possibility made him want to throw up. He looked around the corner into the lounge which was lit only by a single lamp. He took a few more slow steps inside. Thoughts of her being hacked to death by a machete-wielding gangster made his stomach lurch. Images of her hands being chopped off for *muti* invaded his already strained mind.

The lamp shade was tilted at an angle, illuminating a spot on the wall. Taking slow nervous steps, he made his way to the middle of the room and stared at the wall. Sprayed across the wall in red spray paint was,

It's my turn.

*

The sun wasn't due to come up for a few hours. They drove in silence. Red and white lights blotted the horizon. Clouds blocked out the moon. The headlights of cars travelling in the opposite direction broke the darkness for a few seconds but not for long enough to interrupt the darkness which had welled up in his head and his heart. He gripped the steering wheel so hard his knuckles turned white. Natalie sat curled up on the passenger seat beside him, with her feet on the seat, hugging her knees to her chest. She hadn't said a word or uttered a sound since they got into the car. They were both locked into their own minds, alone with their thoughts and pain. But most of all they were alone with their guilt.

"Where are we going?" she asked, after driving in silence for two hours, her voice was muffled and soft.

He didn't answer her.

"Where the hell are we going, Nico?" She turned around in her seat and faced him. Anger, tinged with fear, started to creep into her voice.

The only sound in response to her question was the wind buffeting the car and the engine objecting to the long drive.

"Damn it, Nico. Answer me."

He looked at her for a few seconds and then turned back to the road ahead. He couldn't answer her question. He didn't know where they were going. He had hoped to have come up with a plan by now but all he could see was Janet in the bathtub, with her throat slit and her dead eyes pleading with him to help her.

Natalie pounding her fists against his arm, forced the image out of his mind. Tears were streaming down her cheeks.

"God damn you, Nico. I hate you," she screamed at him. Each time her fist hit his arm, her voice grew louder and more hysterical.

It was a narrow single carriageway with farm land on either side. They had passed the small mining town of Lesley and were half an hour outside of Standerton, a large farming town. There was nothing but farmland between them and

Standerton. He decided that this was as good a spot as any and pulled over into the emergency lane.

"Get out of the fucking car you crazy bitch," his voice was quiet and cold.

"Fuck you." She spat in his face.

He wiped her saliva from his face and dried his hand on her jersey. He got out the car and walked around to her door. She pressed the lock down on her door and then leaned over the driver's seat and locked that door as well.

"Open the door, Natalie," he shouted through the closed window.

She stared straight ahead of her. The only sign that she acknowledged his presence was by extending her middle finger. He took some satisfaction in dangling the car key in front of the window and then proceeded to unlock the car door. Her screams of protest as he pulled her out were shrill and annoying as all hell.

"Shut up," he shouted as he slammed her against the car. "Now, you are going to be a good little psycho and shut up, so I can think. Is that clear?"

She glared at him in silence.

"Is that clear?" He slammed her against the car again.

"Perfectly," she hissed through a clamped jaw.

He let her go and slumped against the car next to her.

They stood in silence for what seemed an eternity. The sun would be up in a few hours. The thought of a new day brought hope that maybe, just maybe, he would be able to kill the bastard without too much damage to himself.

"So genius, we've been standing here like idiots for a while now and I don't know about you, but my arse is numb and I'm cold. I was wondering if you had, by some miracle, any clue as to what we're actually going to do?" Natalie intruded on his thoughts.

"Didn't I tell you to shut up?"

"That was a while ago and if you don't have any ideas I thought you might like to hear mine?"

"Fine! So what's your great idea?"

"We go back to Pretoria. I'll tell you the details on the way."

*

"It just might work," he mumbled to himself.

He couldn't believe that he was going along with Natalie and her crazy idea. Sitting back on his couch after the exhausting round trip to the middle of nowhere, he tried to order her plan in his tired and fumbling mind. It was a dangerous plan and the chances of coming out of it in one piece were slim to none.

Natalie was curled up on the couch opposite him, sleeping soundly. She didn't move in her sleep. The only indication that she was alive was the shallow, yet steady movement of her chest. She had been so calm while telling him about her plan. It was as if all her hysterics from earlier had never happened. Grief and guilt affected people in different ways. If it hadn't been for Janet's murder, Natalie would never have offered to help him to put Louis away. She would probably have protected him to the last, no matter what he did.

He realised then that there must have been a side to Janet that he had never known. How else could she have been close to this woman for so long? Had Janet not seen who and what Natalie really was? Had she not seen that Natalie had serious mental issues? Janet had been many things, but stupid and naïve were not words he would have used to describe her. So how could she not have seen this aspect of her friend? The more he asked himself the questions the less he liked the answers.

Then again, he was going along with her plan. So what did that say about him? Was he just as demented as the man he was trying to bring down?

Natalie's eyes were open and watching him. He realised that he had been staring into space and hadn't noticed that she was awake.

"You certainly were far away," she said with a smirk.

He grunted in reply and got off the couch and walked to the window.

"When are you going?" he asked with his back facing her. The sun was bright and the wind howled and whipped around the building.

"Soon."

"Good, the sooner this is over and done with the better."

"Fine, if that's what you want." She stood up and stretched.

He heard her yawn and then her muffled footsteps made their way across the room to the front door. There was a pause and the door squeaked open and slammed shut.

He would oil the door hinges when this was over.

*

She felt faint with excitement. It was almost over. She had to keep it together for a little while longer. Hell, she just had to survive the next few hours. This time tomorrow she would be free from the guilt and truly alone for the first time since she was a little girl. No Louis and no Janet. She wiped away the tears and forced the pain down, deep inside her. She would deal with it later.

The lift hit the ground floor with a jolt. Her legs felt like rubber under her. She willed them to move. With each step she took her resolve grew stronger. There were moments in the walk towards Johnnie's Café & Bar that she wanted to turn tail and run but she had come too far. She had put too much on the line to stop now. Besides, if she didn't end it her way, Louis would make sure it ended *his* way, which would not be a healthy solution for her or Nico.

The image of Janet in the bloody bathtub squirmed its way into her mind. She tried to shake it, but Janet wouldn't let her go. She didn't want to end up the same way.

"I'm sorry Janet," she said softly. "I'm so sorry."

Her feet crunched on the sandy pathway that led under the trees. The plot of ground across the road from Nico's block of flats was empty except for a few old blue gum trees.

It was a short walk from Nico's flat to Johnnie's Café & Bar, but it felt like an eternity.

The public phone was outside the entrance to the bar. She paused in front of it and took a deep breath before dialling Louis's cell number. She'd left her own cell phone at home in all the craziness.

"Hello." His voice sounded shaky to her ears. She smiled and enjoyed the few beats of silence before answering him.

"So do you miss me?" she asked

"Where are you?"

"That's a nice way to greet me."

"Don't play with me. Just tell me where you are and I'll come get you."

"Impatient, aren't we?"

"Stop your shit and tell me where the fuck you are." His voice grew louder and desperation clung to it like a wet rag. She fought with herself not to burst out laughing. Being so close to her goal made her feel reckless. Her thigh muscles rippled like an excited thoroughbred's before a race. She managed to keep her cool and her voice even.

"I was with Nico."

"With Nico?"

"That's what I said. He's made me feel things I'd never thought possible."

"I'll fucking kill him!" he screamed

"You can try, but I don't think you're man enough." She enjoyed taunting him and his ego made him an easy target.

"Where is he?" He took a new tack and audibly tried to calm himself down.

"Still at his place I would imagine." She could hear his mind ticking over, calculating.

"Natalie, does he know?"

"Know what Louis?"

"Stop with the games. Does he know?"

"Yes, he knows and he's not very happy about it at all. And to be quite honest, neither am I. You really shouldn't have killed Janet."

He exhaled. She heard his breath echo through the

phone line. The phone clicked as she put the handset back in its cradle. Smiling, she walked into the bar and sat on a stool. Johnnie's Café was filled with off-duty or retired cops who had nothing to do except have a beer in the middle of the afternoon. The T.V. above the bar broadcast a local soccer match. The Orlando Pirates were playing Mamelodi Sundowns.

All she had to do now was have a stiff drink while she waited.

*

Nico waited a few minutes after Natalie left before making his phone call.

"SABC," a young woman's voice answered the phone.

"Would you put me through to the Newsroom, please?"

"Just one moment, sir."

He listened to irritating hold music until a harassed-sounding man barked "Newsroom" into the receiver.

"Helen Stratford, please," he asked trying to sound calm.

"Just a sec. Let me see if she's at her desk." There was a pause. "Ok, there she is. Hold on a mo."

The phone rang twice before she picked it up.

"Helen Stratford." Her voice sounded as though elocution lessons were the norm in her daily life. He had found it sexy when they were together, now it just annoyed him.

"Hello Helen." His voice croaked.

"Well, Nico, this is a surprise. What can I do for you?"

"Don't you mean what can I do for you?"

"Very well, Nico. What can you do for me?"

"Be at my place in an hour's time and you'll get that exclusive you've been after." He put the phone down before she could ask him any questions.

He exhaled and sank down on the couch. Putting his elbows on his knees and resting his forehead in the palms of his hands, he wondered if Natalie was setting him up.

*

She looked at the dead phone in her hand as though it were a golden trophy that she had just won after the toughest race in her life. She didn't hear Kyle coming up behind her.

"What's wrong with the phone?"

"Huh," she said, jumping out of her skin. "Don't sneak up on people like that." She put the phone back on its cradle gently.

"Sorry, I didn't realise I was sneaking up on you."

"Just go and pack up your gear."

"Why? What's happening?"

"We have an appointment."

"Who with?"

"With my African Journalist of the year Award. Now stop with the twenty questions and get packed."

"Yes ma'am." He turned and jogged out of the over-crowded open-plan newsroom.

She watched his long legs encased in tatty old jeans and had to admit that he was quite an attractive specimen. When this was over and she had the story in the bag she would be nicer to him, much nicer. Maybe she would make his wildest, wettest fantasies a reality. A blush crept from her neck up to her cheeks as the thought took hold of her body. She savoured the carnal sensation she felt between her legs and fought to control the blush as she put on her tailored jacket. She didn't know which turned her on more: the thought of Kyle or the exclusive story on the Bathroom Strangler and proving to Nico, once and for all, that he did need her.

17

Natalie had left fifteen minutes earlier and he spent that time unproductively. His training was not standing him in good stead. They had trained him to chase after criminals, to build a case against them, put them behind bars and if necessary, shoot them. He had been trained to handle victims and to work a crime scene but what they had failed to teach him was how to take revenge. They had forgotten to train him how to handle it when someone you love is brutally murdered by a madman who wants your attention. They had failed to train him to deal with a woman who was both insane and his only hope.

It took what seemed an eternity before he was able to pull himself together. He stood up, squared his shoulders and set up the tape recorder. He had one more phone call to make. After making his final preparations according to Natalie's strict instructions, he took a beer from the fridge and waited.

*

According to her calculations it was almost time for him to arrive. She left her bar stool and lurked in the doorway which was screened off from the road. She poked her head around the corner of one of the mud-coloured screens and waited.

The wind rustled the leaves on the littered pavement and the TV inside the bar was shouting about the soccer match. The Pirates had scored. She tried to focus on her plan. One of the off-duty cops shouted in frustration at the TV, probably a Sundowns' fan. Natalie wondered if Janet had screamed. Had she known what was happening? Did Janet think that it was her best friend's fault that she was dead? She had done this. It was her fault that Janet was dead. It was her fault that all those women had died by his hand. She'd known what he was and hadn't stopped him. She couldn't blame it all on Louis anymore. The guilt took hold again and Janet's lifeless face stared back at her from the abyss. A part of her knew that what she was feeling was survivor's guilt but the truth was that she'd been too much of a coward to stop him. And there was that element she wished she could silence: the secret desire of hers that had wanted Janet to be punished for her betrayal.

Her cheeks were wet and she realised that she had been crying. Wiping her tears away and hoping that no one had noticed her cry, she struggled with herself and found her resolve to finish what she had started. She owed Janet and all the other women that much. Her neck was starting to spasm when she saw him drive past. It was time to put an end to it once and for all.

*

Heavy footsteps echoed on the hallway tiles outside. Nico gritted his teeth and waited. The knock on the door echoed like a death knell. He took his time getting off the couch, hitting record on the tape recorder and walking across the room to answer it. With each step his feet felt more like lead than flesh and bone. Then again, being made of lead would make this a lot less painful. Hands shaking, heart thumping, he gripped the door knob and took a deep breath to steady himself.

The door creaked on un-oiled hinges as he opened it. The door flew open, the door knob was ripped from his hand. Louis sprang at him with the agility of a cat. A predator going for the kill. Even though he had been expecting this, it still came as a surprise and he struggled to gain control. The door slammed closed. Nico hoped that Natalie had remembered to take the keys. A fist slammed into his gut. Doubling over he stumbled away from Louis.

"Hello Louis, nice of you to drop by," he mumbled between gasps for breath.

Louis strode towards him. He tried to straighten up and was rewarded by a hammer-like fist connecting with his jaw.

"Don't you normally attack drunken old women?" His jaw complained with each word he uttered.

"Shut up." Louis planted a foot in Nico's groin.

He laughed through the pain and rolled onto his hands and knees.

"What's wrong Louis? Can't you kill your mother again?"

Louis' foot lashed out and hit him in the gut, sending him into the back of his couch.

"You don't know a goddamn thing about me. You got suckered by a woman." He gripped Nico by the collar and dragged him towards the bathroom.

"I'm the one who got suckered? I guess we'll know who the sucker is at the end of this."

He got his arm in position and gripped Louis' ankle. Louis stumbled, letting go of him. Nico scrambled to his feet, ready for Louis. His heart beat a staccato in his ears and his lungs burned. Louis leapt to his feet faster than Nico had thought possible.

"Just tell me why, Louis?"

"Why what?" He looked surprised that Nico was asking him questions at a time like this. He started towards Nico.

"Why Janet? Why all those women?" He circled away from Louis, behind the couch.

Louis's laughter was filled with mirth and stopped as suddenly as it had started.

"Because of that *Bitch*," he said as he followed Nico around the room.

"Your mother or Natalie?" Nico kept his eye on Louis and tried to remember where everything was, trying not to fall over anything.

"My loving mother: she made me what I am. Natalie's not a bitch; she just wanted my mother out of our lives for good. Natalie's as much a victim in all of this as I am."

It was now Nico's turn to laugh.

"So this is all your mother's fault? And you're totally innocent in all of this."

"Of course it's her fault. You're lucky you didn't have a mother like mine."

"What about Janet?"

They kept waltzing around the couch.

171

"What about her?"

"Was it your mother's fault that you killed Janet?"

"No, that was your fault. And there was the fact that she was just like them … I did the world a favour when I killed my fucking mother … those women were all the same. Drunken whores just like *her*."

"Janet wasn't like that."

"She was a whore and would have ended up just like them. I did you both a favour by putting her out of her misery before she drank you both down the drain." His smile was evil. "Did she tell you that she liked me to fuck her up the arse?"

"You lying bastard." Nico launched himself across the room and tackled Louis. His fist landed against Louis's hard stomach. Breath escaped from between clenched teeth. Louis was on top. How did that happen? Nico asked himself through the haze that was clouding his mind. One fist after the other connected with his stomach. A fist hit his jaw. He closed his mind to the pain.

His body was being dragged but he was no longer in control of it. The bathroom tiles felt cool to the touch. So this is it, he thought. They won't be here in time. Hands gripped his shirt and pulled him to his knees. The bathroom was dark and cold. An icy grip settled on his body. He welcomed the end. Tired and beaten, he knelt on the hard tiled floor and stared at the closed door wondering who would be the one to find him. Louis stood behind him.

"I'm going to enjoy this." Louis whispered into his ear, as he looped the wire over his head. He felt the wire scratch his skin as it was pulled tighter. "I'm going to take it nice and slow." Louis's voice was low and husky with excitement. Hot blood trickled slowly down his throat. Eyes closed, he waited for it to end. He was tired.

Janet beckoned from the abyss.

Loud banging jolted him from the edge. Someone kicked the bathroom door. The wire tightened with each bang. The bathroom grew darker with each trickle of blood that left his body.

"Louis," Natalie screamed from the other side of the door. "Open this fucking door now."

The door swung open, splintered at the lock. Pete burst in brandishing his pistol. Natalie stood behind him.

A shot rang out and the wire loosened. He fell back. The ceiling needed another coat of paint he decided as the lights went out.

*

The SABC News van was parked outside the entrance. Natalie recognised Helen immediately. Janet had described her as a barracuda and it suited her quite well. Pete stood behind Natalie. They were under the yellow awning at the entrance to Nico's block and watched the paramedics carry Nico out on a stretcher.

"He won't be able to wear any v-neck shirts anymore," Pete said, as they slid the stretcher into the ambulance. He sounded drained.

"No, I guess he won't. I'll buy him a polo neck for his birthday," Natalie said, staring at the ambulance. Now that it was over and she had her revenge, she felt empty inside.

"Nico said you had something for me," Pete said, still staring at the ambulance.

"He did?"

"*Ja*. When he called me he said you had a package for me."

"Oh, *ja*," she said and fumbled in her bag and pulled out a plastic sandwich bag with a memory card in it. "This was Louis's. It's got all the photos of his victims on it and you'll find his finger prints on it as well." She then handed him Nico's tape recorder. "You'll also be needing this. It's Louis's confession."

"Thanks. Well, I guess I'd better go and give Ms Witch Stratford over there her interview before Laurel and Hardy show up and give their version of events. What are you going to do now?"

"I'm going to go to the hospital and wait for him to wake

up," she said and walked towards the ambulance. She climbed inside the back with Nico and held his hand.

*

The lights were bright and burned his eyes through his closed eyelids. His fingers explored the surface he was lying on. It was soft and smooth. He was warm and in agony. Every muscle hurt. One eye opened slowly and painfully. He tried to distinguish different shapes and objects through the haze of little lights flashing in front of him. He blinked. That didn't work.

"Nurse," a woman's voice, which sounded suspiciously like Natalie's, shouted next to him. It reverberated though his head, bouncing against the back of his skull.

"I think he's waking up." The woman's voice was softer this time. He opened his eye again, only to have a bright light shone into it. He closed it quickly, trying to shut out the pain that was shooting through his brain.

A soft hand gripped his hand tightly.

"Hold on. You're going to be okay. Just hold on." The woman's voice was at his ear, whispering softly. He felt soft hair touch his face. The smell of apples drifted gently up his nose. He opened his eye and tried to focus on the woman standing over him. All he could make out was long, dark hair.

He closed his eyes and drifted off to sleep, knowing that Natalie had kept her side of the deal.

About the Author

Joan De La Haye writes horror and some very twisted thrillers. She invariably wakes up in the middle of the night, because she's figured out yet another freaky way to mess with her already screwed up characters.

Joan is interested in some seriously weird shit. That's probably also one of the reasons she writes horror.

Joan is deep, dark and seriously twisted and so is her writing.

http://joandelahaye.com/

21786808R10103

Made in the USA
Charleston, SC
30 August 2013